The Gree

Book Three

Old Sins Cast Long Shadows

M. KATHERINE CLARK

For my family, friends, and fans.

And a special thank you to my eight grade science teacher who planned a forensic lab for us and had us write up a story in order to solve it. These characters started then. Thank you so much!

Other Works by M. Katherine Clark

The Greene and Shields Files:

    Blood is Thicker Than Water

    Once Upon a Midnight Dreary

    Old Sins Cast Long Shadows

    Tales from the Heart, Novelettes

Soundless Silence a Sherlock Holmes Novel

The Rest is Silence, an Edmond Holmes Novel – Coming Soon

Love Among the Shamrocks Collection:

    Under the Irish Sky

    Across the Irish Sea

    On the River Shannon

    The Land Across the Sea, an Emmet O'Quinn Short

Love Among the Shamrocks Collection, the Next Generation:

    In Dublin Fair City

    The Song of Heart's Desire

    Chasing After Moonbeams – Coming Soon

The Wolf's Bane Saga:

    Wolf's Bane

    Lonely Moon

    Midnight Sky

    Star Crossed

    Moon Rise

    Moon Song, a Companion Guide

Silent Whispers, a Scottish Ghost Story

Dragon Fire

    Heart of Fire

    Will of Fire – Coming Soon

Prologue

Zoe stumbled to her car, the blinding pain blurring her already clouded vision. Her hands shook as she tried three times to get the damn keys in the ignition. Finally, the old ford started up.

The moon's rays were obscured by the snow clouds and the white flakes shown in her headlights. Her car swerved when the worn tires hit a patch of black ice.

The pain in her side grew more intense. She had to get help. Pulling out her cell phone, she dialed a number only to hear nothing as the call couldn't connect to a tower. Looking at the screen, she cursed the No Service icon at the top.

Cursing in frustration, she leaned over, crying out when her side collided with the gear shift. The satellite phone was in the glove compartment. It rang. Rang. And rang.

"Dammit, answer!" she shouted.

"Zoe?" his voice came over the receiver.

"Finally! Listen, Skylark is blown. He knows, Steven. He –
shit!" she screamed when she saw the oncoming headlights of an
eighteen-wheeler.

"Zoe? Zoe!" Steven shouted.

VIKTOR REDORVSKY SHOT DEAD BY POLICE

IND – Viktor Redorvsky, son of Russian businessman Viktor Demetrovich Redorvsky, was shot dead by police yesterday while walking home with a friend. According to eye witnesses, Redorvsky, 18, was walking along the alleyway between Chatham Tap and his friend's apartment complex. Redorvsky and his unnamed friend were then swarmed by IMPD officers and a firefight ensued. Redorvsky was shot dead and his friend was wounded. Redorvsky's father was subsequently arrested by the Organized Crime division of the IMPD. His hearing is set for later this month. Police are asking anyone with any information to please step forward and inform the IMPD.

Chapter One

Viktor rubbed his eyes as the words of the article on his laptop blurred. He looked at the clock in the bottom corner and yawned. Before he could shut the laptop down, there was a knock at his bedroom door.

"Who is it?" He called.

"Keelan," a voice said.

"Come in," Viktor replied.

The door opened and Keelan O'Grady leaned against the doorframe.

"Still worried your father will find you?" He asked.

Viktor shrugged. "Force of habit."

"Are you all right?"

"Couldn't sleep," Viktor admitted closing the lid of his laptop.

"Jet lag after a month?" Keelan asked.

"No," he answered. "Something else."

"What's wrong, Greg?" Keelan asked.

"Couldn't you call me Vitya?" Viktor asked. "I mean, I appreciate my new life but I miss being called by my real name."

Keelan shook his head. "Probably wouldn't be best," he stated. "Viktor Viktorovich Redorvsky is dead, remember?"

"Yeah. It's strange seeing my obituary," Viktor sighed.

"What's wrong?" Keelan asked. "Are you homesick?"

"It's hard to be homesick when you've never had a home," he answered.

"I can tell something's on your mind, lad," Keelan said. "You know you can tell me anything."

Viktor sighed and opened his laptop. Keelan pushed off the doorway and sat on the side of the bed.

"This," Viktor said as he played a news video.

An older man was speaking outside a courthouse in front of several reporters.

"These police have made mistake. I am an honest businessman," Viktor heard his father's Russian accented voice and suppressed a shudder. "They arrested me on word of two men who have, for some reason, disappeared and cannot be found. The judge had no choice but to let me go. And these police will see just how powerful I truly am."

"Mr. Redorvsky, is it true that one of your arresting officers killed your son Viktor last month?" One of the reporters asked.

Redorvsky stopped and looked at the reporter.

"My son was innocent and not given fair trial. The cop who shot him will pay. They will all pay…" he looked directly into the camera. "I know who you are. I will find you. You cannot escape me. I will return favor."

Detective Courtney Shields woke in a panic, her heart racing, sweat making her hair stick to her neck. Looking around the darkened room, she tried to calm her ragged heartbeat. Her recurrent dream since her time beneath the sharpened pendulum was still vivid in her mind. Swallowing, she took another deep breath.

"Courtney?" Ryan's voice came from beside her. Looking over, she took his hand as he reached toward her. "Are you okay, baby?"

She shook her head. Predawn light broke through her bedroom window outlining Ryan's silhouette as he lay on his stomach. Moving slightly, he leaned up on his elbow and stroked her face.

"What's wrong?" he asked.

"I keep having a dream," she replied.

He sat up fully and her eyes went down to his bare chest. Taking her in his arms, he slowly stroked her back.

"What sort of dream?" he asked.

"I'm back at the warehouse, under the pendulum," she

answered. "And I can't get out."

"But you did," he said. "You did get out."

"I know," she replied. "But it doesn't help."

"What can I do?" he asked.

"You've already done it," she said. "Just by being here."

Slowly, he leaned them both back on the bed and held her tightly.

"Do you want to talk to someone?" Ryan asked. "Uncle Jon swears by his shrink. Maybe you could talk to him?"

"That might not be a bad idea," she replied.

"Did you talk to the Police Psychiatrist?" he asked.

"Yeah, but it didn't seem to help," she said.

"It's not been long enough," he replied. "You need more time."

Nodding, she stroked the fine hairs on his chest.

"I'm glad you're here," she said. "I'm glad we're together."

His arms tightened around her and he kissed her hair.

"Me too," he answered. "You aren't worried we didn't wait?"

"We waited long enough," she replied. "I needed you that night and you were there. I don't think I could face this without you."

"Me too, baby. Are you sure you want to go back? Maybe you could call Dave and tell him you're not ready."

"You can't take another sick day to be with me," she snuggled deeper into him. "And I need to get back out there. I've had nearly a month off. I need to get back to it."

"I'm here if you want or need me," he replied.

"I always want you," she teased looking up at him. Shimming her way up to be eye level with him, she kissed his lips and distracted them both until the alarm on his phone went off. Groaning, he tapped it quiet. "Do you really have to go in?" she pouted as he rolled out of bed and grabbed his clothes.

"You just told me not an hour ago that I couldn't take any more time off," he laughed.

"I know, but that was before you distracted me," she replied.

"And I would distract you again," he knelt on the bed and leaned forward. "If I didn't have an ER filled with patients."

"And they are all in need of your special attention," she said. "As I am."

"That is completely different special attention and I plan on lavishing you with it as soon as you get home," he said.

"Home? I don't recall inviting you over tonight," she answered.

"You didn't," he teased. "I just thought I would help you out and invite myself."

"And what if I wanted to invite another hot doctor home for the evening?" she asked.

"You'd have a hard time finding a hotter one," he kissed her.

"That's true," Courtney laughed, then, smacking his shoulder, she continued. "Go, take a shower, before I tie you to my bed."

"Don't tempt me," he winked.

"Go, I'll get coffee going."

"I love you," he said softly. "And I want you to call me if you can't do today, okay?"

"I will but I'll be fine, baby," she replied. "Jon will be there and Dave so I'll have all the protection you could hope for me. I need to get back. I need to do something."

"I know you do," he said. "Just be careful."

"I'll call you when I have a break, okay?" she offered.

"Perfect," he replied. "And I'm making dinner tonight."

"I love your short shifts," she teased.

"Me too," he answered.

"Any word on the promotion you interviewed for two months ago?" She asked.

"Nothing yet," he replied. "Fred said it could take a couple months. They have to make a show of interviewing other candidates," grinning, he raised his hands in innocence. "His words not mine."

"Assistant Head of Surgery," Courtney whistled low. "Sexy."

"Yeah, it is," he teased. "I'd be working with Fred most of the time so it's not like I don't know how to handle him."

"He's a good guy," she said.

"He is," Ryan agreed. "I gotta jump in the shower. I love you." Kissing her once more before heading to the bathroom, he flicked on the overhead vent and light.

Courtney listened to the sound of the water gushing and

then the shower start. For a moment, she reveled in Ryan's love. After their first time together, they agreed not to tell anyone. She wasn't ashamed but she wanted to keep the newness and forbidden desires to herself.

But when the memory of her would-be-shower-garrotter from last month came back to her, Courtney allowed herself five seconds to get through the fear as the police shrink told her. Taking a deep breath, she stood, grabbed one of Ryan's oversized sweatshirts he had given her and headed to the kitchen. Brewing a pot of coffee, she was nearly done with his omelet when Ryan walked out dressed in his usual suit.

"Damn, I love you," he teased kissing the back of her neck, exposed by the sloppy bun she had pulled her hair into.

"You are lucky," she replied.

"I know I am," he poured two cups of coffee and grabbed the hazelnut creamer from the refrigerator. Making a latté for them both, he watched her move about in bare feet and nothing but his old Notre Dame sweatshirt. "You are making it very difficult to want to go to work today."

"That's my job," she swayed to the music playing in the background on her vinyl record player. "Besides I have to keep you away from all those pretty little nurses."

"Which do you mean? Maybe Mrs. Reed? Oh, I know! Mrs. Phillips, the lady who is old enough to be my great grandmother."

"Mmhmm," Courtney teased. "I've had my eye on her for a long time. It's always the quiet ones."

"I'm gonna have to tell her you said that," he said. "She'll get a kick out of it."

"Tell her I know exactly what her plan is, playing the sweet little old lady act," she bit her lip. Ryan saddled up behind her, pulled her tightly against him and kissed her neck.

"I like this little jealous streak of yours," he whispered in her ear making her shudder. "But you don't have to worry about Mrs. Reed or old Mrs. Phillips, why would I want them, when I have you to come home to? You are my life, Courtney Shields, and soon you will be my wife." Turning in his arms, she wrapped hers around his neck.

"And you are mine, Ryan Marcellino," she answered. "You have seen me at my best and my worst and you are still here. I love you."

"And I," he kissed the tip of her nose. "Love you."

"You better, now, would you eat this delicious omelet before it gets cold?"

"Wouldn't want that," grinning, he broke away from her and straddled a kitchen barstool, watching as she cut the omelet in half placing one half on her plate and the other on his.

Chapter Two

Sitting in her car, looking at the elevators leading to her precinct, Courtney took a deep breath. It had been nearly a month since she had stepped into that elevator and even now the nerves built inside her. She was a good cop, but after something so devastating, so traumatizing, she wasn't sure she was ready to return. One more deep breath, she breathed in the eucalyptus scented car freshener Ryan bought her. It calmed her and gave her courage.

Grabbing her handbag, keys, the two coffees and the two dozen donuts she had stopped to get, she locked her car and walked briskly to the doors.

"Hold the elevator!" she called as it started to close. A hand shot out and stopped the door from closing. "Thanks." She breathed then looked at her elevator mate. "Scott? Oh my god, what are you doing here? Are you in court?" Giving him a quick awkward hug with her hands full, she made sure not to spill the coffees on his Armani suit.

"Hey, Courtney," her partner's son replied, offering to take the donuts for her. "Dad said it was going to be your first day back. How are you doing?"

"Great," she answered. "Feeling better at least."

"Good," he grinned. "I get it, you know? If you ever need someone to talk to, let me know. I'm here for you."

"Thank you," she answered. "I will probably take you up on that."

"That cousin of mine taking care of you?" he asked.

"Completely," she answered. "But, how are you? What are you doing here?"

"I'm feeling great. The doc says I'm back to ninety percent rotary function."

"That's fantastic!" she cried.

"And the wedding is nearly planned," he replied. "Kim is a saint putting up with my work schedule. There's been a shit load to do; I'm lucky if I make it home by midnight."

"That's tough, but she loves you so it's easy," she stated. "Are you in court today?"

"You could say that," he answered. "Dad wants to sit in on the Redorvsky hearing so I volunteered to join him."

"That's nice of you," she replied.

"Hey, it's a free lunch," he teased. The elevator dinged as she laughed and they both stepped out. Applause greeted her as they rounded the corner into the bullpen. Shock changed to a soft smile as Courtney thanked them for their welcome back. Jon and Dave stepped out of their offices joining in the applause. Finally, after everyone quieted down and she showed Scott where to put the donuts, she reached her partner and boss.

"Hey, kid, you look great," Dave started. "How do you feel?"

"Nearly one hundred percent," she replied. Once the door to their office was closed, she handed them both a coffee and hugged them.

"It's been quiet and peaceful without you here," Dave teased. "There's no one to raise hell."

"Gotta keep you on your toes," she retorted. "And here I thought about calling in sick."

"You could have, there's nothing pressing to do," Jon replied. "Scott and I are heading over to sit in on Redorvsky's hearing. You're welcome to join us."

"Oh, no thanks," she answered. "I think I'll get a start on stuff here."

"If you're sure," Jon replied.

"Bad luck it falls on the same day you return," Dave tsked.

"Oh, come on guys," Courtney started. "It's not like I'm going to run off."

"Right, well," Jon began. "Thank you for the coffee. I'll be back up as soon as it's over."

"You guys go, go to lunch," Courtney said. "You've earned it." An uncomfortable pause built around them until Scott spoke.

"Hey Dave, you had that thing you wanted to show me in your office, didn't you?"

"I did?" Dave asked. Then after a beat, he nodded. "Oh, right that thing. Yeah, come on. I'll be happy to show it to you."

Jon looked down as the men left the room and chuckled silently.

"Wow, not very subtle, were they?" Courtney asked.

"My son, the man who thinks he knows what's best for everyone but himself," Jon replied. Turning to her, he held her gaze for a long moment.

"You cut your hair," she said.

"Yeah," he admitted. "I was ready for a new look. They cut a little too much on the sides but I like it, so does Beth."

"That's good. I like it too."

"Thanks," Jon replied. "Really, how are you?"

"It's been a month, Jon," she shrugged. "When I said we needed a break, I didn't expect you to take it so literally."

"I wanted to give you and Ryan time. I remember what it was like to be newly together," he replied.

"You know?" she asked.

"It's kinda hard not to," he answered. "I am pleased for you both."

"But I don't understand why you kept your distance from me. Ryan has told me you had him over several times and met him for lunch. You never once reached out to me," she said.

"Because I didn't want to influence you," he answered. "We

said some pretty damning things, Courtney. I needed to make sure our feelings were merely because we are in the line of fire together and we depend on each other."

"And were they?" she asked.

"My phone wasn't ringing off the hook either. You have to understand, as much as things will be the same between us, things are different now and we have to work through them. I think it's a good thing you and Ryan are together, it shows he is where your heart truly lies."

She looked up at him and finally whispered. "But I missed you."

Jon sighed and pulled her into him tightly. "God, I missed you too. But I couldn't do that to you or Ryan. We needed space."

"And now we've had it, and now I am fully with Ryan," she said into his chest. "I know my... infatuation caused a lot of chaos. I'm sorry. I do love you, Jon but not like that. We're partners. I think a partnership is a lot like and can be confused for a relationship but that's not what I want with you."

"I don't either, to be honest," Jon replied. "I'll admit there was a time when we first met I thought what if, but it was brief. Courtney, I have, at times, projected my late wife onto you and it's not fair to either of us. I think that's why your confession was so difficult for me. It was like I was losing Carol all over again. But you are not Carol and I am so very happy with Beth as you are with Ryan. Can we leave it and see where we go from here?

"Yes," Courtney nodded. "I realized after I said it, it was

childish and I have strived for so long to make everyone see me as an adult but I realized I couldn't be who I wanted to be living in a fantasy world. I thought I knew what love was but now I do and I realized what I felt for you was infatuation, admiration and companionship."

"That is partly my fault. I pretended for a while Carol was back. I know now that was a wish and desire I had no business putting on you. Can we go on from here?"

"Gladly, partner," Courtney beamed and squeezed his hands in hers.

"Now, I do have to go. I'm going to be late. How about tonight, when we're off duty, we go to Chatham Tap for a Guinness?" Jon asked.

"Oh, I would, but Ryan is making dinner tonight," she answered. "Raincheck?"

"Knocked out for my younger, cuter nephew, eh?" he shook his head dramatically.

Courtney threw her head back and laughed. "If you think of it that way then we've not made any progress."

"True," he winked. "But truthfully, how are you?"

"That conversation will take more time than the five seconds we have until Scott comes back through that door and tells us you're going to be late," she said and sure enough Scott popped his head in from Dave's office.

"If you two are finished, we're going to be late, Dad," he announced.

"You really are pushy when there's a free lunch in it for you," Jon said.

"Of course," his son teased. "I'm a growing boy."

"Growing boy, my arse," Jon answered.

———◦◦———

"You cannot escape me. I will return favor," Redorvsky said into the camera.

Jon stood on the steps of the courthouse with his hands in his suit pants pocket as Scott walked up beside him.

"I still can't believe it, dad," Scott said. "The prosecution had an ironclad case, they presented it well," he shook his head. "I just don't get how the judge could let him off."

Jon didn't move as he watched Redorvsky get into his black suburban and drive away.

"We have a lot of work to do," Jon finally replied.

"What do you need?" Scott asked.

"I need you to ask around about Judge Cross. Ask your colleagues if he's been fair in other trials."

"You think Cross is in Redorvsky's pocket?" Scott asked.

"Every man has his price," Jon said.

"I've worked with him a number of times, I pray you're wrong. What are you going to do?"

"I need to think," Jon said and walked down the steps.

Scott looked after him. "Great," he said to himself. "What about lunch?"

Chapter Three

Courtney sat in her office staring at more paperwork. The forms were starting to run together and it took her four tries to read one sentence. Ghosts and shadows of the last time she was in the precinct lingered in her mind.

Contemplating texting Ryan to meet up for a quick lunch, she pulled her phone out of her handbag and unlocked the screen. Tapping out a quick message to reply to the two he had sent earlier, she waited on requesting a lunch date. She had to stand on her own.

Leaning back in her chair, she looked toward the window to her right and saw the blue sky and wispy clouds on the bright May morning. Early summer was in full swing and for Indiana that meant anywhere from ninety degree heat to forty degree freeze. Having spent a lot of her downtime outside at the advice of the police shrink, Courtney missed curling up with a good book and sitting with a glass of wine or a cup of coffee on her balcony without a care of pits or pendulums.

Always a fan of Edgar Allan Poe, she was thrilled when his stories seemed to be coming to life on the streets of Indianapolis. But when she became the star player in her favorite story, the thrill decidedly evaporated and merely the thought of survival kicked in. The police shrink said it would take time for her to work through her body responding in a fight or flight even when nothing was happening. Her parents were wonderful helping her through the dark times, and Ryan was a saint. But as she sat at her desk, the same desk she sat at when she figured it was Poe, the same desk, the same set up, the same everything, she wanted to pull her hair out and scream.

Her heart rate kicked up three notches and her palms began to sweat as she clutched the paper in her hand tighter, wrinkling the pages. Everything intensified, every sound around her, every voice, every tap of the keyboard keys from outside in the bullpen, was as if it was in her head. Deep breaths. She tried to take deep breaths but all she felt was the restrictions from the ropes and the sheer terror she felt when she heard the swoosh of the pendulum swinging above her.

Shrieking when a delivery man's dolly skidded across the old linoleum making a grating metallic sound, she shot from her chair and raced to the window with the express purpose of opening the non-opening window. The noise of the water cooler refills the man was delivering as they slapped on top of each other had her reaching for her gun.

Visions of Paul Anderson dressed as the Masque of Red Death, danced in her mind and the musty smell of the old warehouse that was to be her scene of death filled her nose.

Someone was trying the door to her office.

Pointing the gun at whoever was coming in, she cried out when the door opened and would have fired her weapon had that person not had concerned but kind blue eyes. Dave raced over to her and grabbed the gun out of her hands, clutching her to his chest.

She always had a soft spot for her instructor in the academy and, as she came to find out, Homeland Security's best undercover operative in the greater Midwest. She clutched at his oxford shirt and buried her head into his chest. Shaking uncontrollably, her heart beat rapidly.

"Shh shh, it's all right, you're all right," she finally heard Dave say. His lips had been moving for a little while but her ringing ears couldn't hear what he was saying. "You're safe. You're fine. Everything is all right."

"Dave," she breathed finally looking up at him.

"Yeah, hey there," he said softly, moving her hair out of her face. "You're okay."

Finally taking a deep breath, she swallowed and tried to calm her heartbeat. Once she looked up into Dave's eyes, the episode had passed.

"Dave," she whispered. "I'm sorry."

"No, no, you have nothing to be sorry about," he said. "I had a feeling it was too soon for you to come back. You've had a trauma."

"PTSD the shrink said," she agreed.

"I shouldn't have pushed you into coming back before you were ready," he said.

"You didn't," she countered. "You encouraged me to stay home. I *wanted* to come back, Dave. I *had* to come back. Sitting at home was great but in order to conquer it, truly conquer it, I had to be here." She pushed away from him slightly and stood. "I'm only sorry it was during working hours. I should have been in more control."

"You were like this at the academy you know," he shook his head. "Always trying too hard to push yourself to your breaking point. Everyone has limits, Courtney. They're not something to be ashamed of or to fight. You went through hell and it's going to take a lot longer than a couple weeks to get you feeling better."

"Don't send me away, Dave," Courtney said. "Give me something to do. I will truly lose my mind if I stay home any longer."

"Fine," he huffed a sigh and ran his hand along one side of his military buzz haircut. "But nothing too dangerous."

At that moment, an announcement came over the PA system.

All downtown units, we have a person shot at 15 North Alabama courtroom steps. Special deputies are asking for assistance as the perpetrator is no longer in the courthouse.

Courtney's eyes lit with the fire Dave missed. Rushing to his desk, Dave dialed dispatch "What's the situation?" he spoke into the phone and waited. "Is the sheriffs' department on the scene? Close off the block and create a one-mile perimeter, I want check points at all major intersections. I am sending my best." Dave hung up the phone and turned to Courtney who stood tall.

"One fatality," he said. "A judge. Suspect fled the scene in a black SUV. Several witnesses."

"Is Jon already on the scene?"

"No," he answered. "But Scott is."

Courtney's eyes grew large then she tampered down her expression. "Is he all right?"

"He's the main witness. I'm going out on a limb here, Shields," he said. "At the risk of sounding callous, I cannot have you having a nervous breakdown in the field."

"You will not, sir, I am in control," she stated.

"And earlier?" he indicated the window.

"An error in judgement," she replied.

"I better not regret this, Shields," he sighed. "Call your partner and check in with me every half hour."

"I will, Sir," she answered.

"Go," he ordered. "But at the merest hint…"

"Jon will be the first to know, then you."

"Good."

———◦◦◦———

Judge Connor Cross closed his chambers door quickly, his hands shaking as he pulled out his phone and dialed a number.

"I've done what you asked," he said when they answered. "You promised you'd let her go."

"I am a man of my word, Mr. Cross," the man said. "Your daughter is on the courthouse steps."

Connor took off running. Rushing out of his chambers, down the hall, up the stairs and out the main door, he nearly collided with Scott.

"Ah, Your Honor," Scott smiled. "Scott Greene; Greene, Moore and Anderson attorneys, I was in the courtroom today. I was wondering if I could—"

"I'm sorry, Counselor," Cross said. "I'm in a bit of a hurry." He pushed past Scott and ran down the stairs, looking around frantically. A black suburban pulled out of a metered parking spot and slowly drove up to the steps.

Connor pulled out his phone and dialed the same number from earlier.

"Where is she?" He demanded.

"Dear oh dear, I didn't say *which* courthouse, did I?" the man mocked. "Thank you for your cooperation today, Your Honor. It is appreciated. You will see your daughter again very soon."

The suburban rolled down the back window.

Chapter Four

Scott heard the shots and immediately ducked. Tires squealed and people screamed, but when it was quiet again, he lifted his head and saw Judge Cross lying on the steps. Rushing towards him, Scott yelled to one of the aids beside him.

"Call 911!" When he reached the judge, he tore off his jacket and used it to apply pressure against the wounds in his chest. "Your Honor, can you hear me?" The judge was still alive as he shakily looked up at Scott. "You're going to be okay."

"Donna," he wheezed.

"Sir?" Scott asked.

Motioning him down, Cross whispered in his ear. "They have Donna... forced me... let him off."

"What?" Scott pulled back and searched his face. Conner's eyes rolled back in his head as blood spilled out of his mouth. "No, come on, stay with me, Judge," Scott called to him. The judge's eyelids fluttered closed just as Scott began CPR and heard sirens in the distance.

"What have we got?" Jon ducked under the police tape and headed over to his partner.

"Judge Conner Cross," Courtney answered standing from the body on the steps. "Two GSWs to the chest, death followed before EMS got here."

"He was the judge for Redorvsky," Jon revealed.

"Crooked?" she asked.

"I asked Scott to check around," he answered.

"Well, Scott is the main witness and the Good Samaritan who administered CPR," Courtney replied. When her partner's gaze flew to hers, she continued. "He's fine, getting checked out in the ambulance. I have everything here, you go."

Immediately, Jon headed toward the ambulance Courtney had indicated and rounded the corner to see Scott sitting on the back step.

"Scott," Jon breathed. His son looked up.

"Hey," he replied.

"You okay?" Jon asked, his eyes passing over him from the blood on his shirt to the blood pressure cuff still strapped to his arm.

"Yeah," Scott answered and looked up when the EMT removed the medical device. Rolling up the opposite sleeve of his dress shirt to match, he stepped down and stood in front of his father. "A little shaken but I'm good."

"You sure?" Jon asked.

"Yeah," Scott replied. "Just um…" he broke off and took a deep breath. "The EMTs wanted to check me out. They're Ryan's friends."

"Thank you," Jon called up to the burly former Notre Dame Football player. The man nodded and turned to a woman being administered oxygen for an asthma attack. "What happened?"

"Not altogether sure," Scott answered walking with him back toward the police tape. "When you left, I texted a friend about Cross and asked him out to lunch to speak more. He had just texted back when Judge Cross came running out." They stopped at the police tape and Scott went on explaining what happened.

"I hate it when I'm right," Jon rubbed his hands down his face.

"Me too," Scott sighed. "If he is corrupt, then a lot of his cases will have to be reopened."

"What about the name; Donna?" Jon asked.

"No idea. Wife? Daughter, maybe?" Scott replied.

"I'll have it run," Jon assured. "Want to go home?"

"Yeah, I wanna burn this shirt and could use a drink," Scott said.

"We need to take your statement, then go," he said and indicated the uniform officer walking up. "Take his statement, if you would." He instructed the officer, then turned back to his son. "I'll be home later. Be careful."

"I will," Scott promised.

"I got your message. What happened?" CIA Special Agent Steven Anderson entered the apartment loft and slipped off his painter's overalls.

Agent Brent Tyler looked up from the monitors and his bowl of caramel popcorn.

"Cross is dead," he announced.

"Shit," Steven replied, then looked over to the bedroom door as Zoe, another of his agents, walked out.

"What do you mean Cross is dead?" she asked.

"Somebody shot him on the steps of the courthouse," Brent went on.

"Who's the cop in charge?" Steven asked

"Jonathan Greene," Brent answered.

"Oh no no," Steven breathed, leaning forward and peering at the security feed. "Dammit, what are you doing, Jon?"

"Should we change the plan?" Zoe asked.

"No," Steven said. "There's too much at stake here. We've put too much manpower into this. Zoe, get to Minneapolis, we need you on O'Malley. Brent, meet up with Danny and keep eyes on Redorvsky."

"Where is our resident Irishman?" Brent asked.

"Doing recon," Steven revealed. "He's following

Redorvsky's car. He'll check in later."

"What do you want us to do with Greene and Shields?" Brent asked.

"Nothing," Steven answered. "I'll handle them."

"Steven," Zoe walked up to them. "You're not in the field any longer. After you took Gordon down and got his job, you are, figuratively, in the van."

"Zo," Steven turned to her. "I'll never be in the van. Okay? I may be your handler but I'll always be in the field. That's where Gordon screwed up. I'm not him. We'll all have to adjust to this but that's what's happening. Now, get your mark. Skylark is a go."

Chapter Five

"How is he?" Courtney asked as Jon walked up the courthouse steps and Scott headed in the direction of the parking garage.

"A little shaken," Jon admitted.

"Yeah, I can imagine, especially after what he's been through," she said.

"How are you doing?" Jon asked.

"I wasn't here," she answered and crouched down lifting the tarp covering the body. "I'm sure I'd be just as bad off as he is if I were. But since I'm not, let's get to work."

Jon nodded once. "Then give me the run down."

"Judge Connor Cross," Courtney started. "Sixty-four, Chicago native, been at the bar for forty years, twenty of which he was on the bench."

"He let Redorvsky off," Jon explained.

"And we're operating on the idea Redorvsky was using him and he was killed because he outlived his usefulness?"

"Sounds about right," Jon stated. "But I want to explore the possibility Redorvsky held something over him. Scott said Judge Cross said the name Donna before he died. Run it and see what bites."

"Got it, anything else?" She asked taking notes.

"Yeah, we need to call Ireland," Jon stated.

"I'm guessing not to check in on your mom," Courtney replied.

Scott's hand shook as he set his keys down on the washroom ledge. Adrenaline still pumped through his veins and as soon as the door closed behind him, his legs buckled and he fell against the wall. Letting out a cry, he embraced the fear for ten seconds; it was all he would allow. His shoulder ached with the memory of a bullet tearing through his muscle and flesh. Focusing his mind on something else as the psychiatrist had suggested, he thought of Kim. His fiancée's face, her laugh, he even went so far as to remember her moans as they made love. With those thoughts, the fear ebbed enough. He stood and headed to the bar, pouring a glass of whiskey.

Unbuttoning his shirt, he pulled it off and took a gulp of the liquor. Setting his drink down, he stripped out of his t-shirt and flipped off his shoes. Heading upstairs, he ran a shower. Allowing the hot water to run over him, he took a deep breath of the minty bath soap. After he was shot, Scott's usual body wash irritated his wound. Mint was new but comforting.

"Scott?" he heard his dad call. Looking up through the steam, his brow furrowed.

"Dad?" he called back. He wasn't sure how long had he been in the shower.

"Courtney and I needed to call Ireland, we're downstairs," he said.

"Okay," he replied. "Oh, dad?"

"Yeah?" Jon said through the door.

"Can you call Kim for me?" he asked. "I don't want to bother you guys and I don't—"

"I gotcha," Jon cut him off. "I'm calling her now."

"Thanks."

Keelan, Viktor, and Jon's mother Kathleen sat in the family dining room in Alleen Caiseal after dinner, laughing until tears ran down their cheeks.

"Oh, I haven't laughed like that in… well forever," Viktor said wiping his eyes.

"Me neither," Keelan answered. "At least not for a long time. Thank you."

"Who would like a wee glass of whiskey?" Kathleen asked standing.

"I'll take one," Keelan answered. "I need to be up early, though so a small one. There have been reports of an issue with the out pasture."

"How are things?" Kathleen asked opening the decanter.

"As far as I know, manageable," he answered. "But I haven't inspected the latest damage. That last storm we had did a number on the crofts."

"I meant with you and Aislín," she said delicately, handing him his drink.

"Oh," he breathed. "Not good. Her sister has somewhat warned me to prepare for the worst."

"But why?" Viktor asked then looked up at Kathleen as she handed him a whiskey. "Thanks," he smiled and looked back at Keelan. "Why would she want a divorce?"

"We've been apart for the past several years. Since Riley first was assumed dead it took everything to keep our marriage together. And now we've lost both Riley and Brendan... I don't think there is anything I can do to help her heal."

"But I don't understand," Viktor went on. "If she really loved you wouldn't she try to make it work?"

"You've brought up a very interesting point. *If* she really loved me... Well," he glanced over at Kathleen and looked down. "Our marriage was made out of necessity not love."

"We all knew Colman was conceived before your marriage, Keelan," Kathleen answered. "You did the honorable thing."

"But I don't think we ever really loved each other," Keelan

admitted. "We were kids, your age in fact, Greg," he looked at Viktor. "We didn't know what we were doing and we had no business getting married."

There was a knock on the door and Kathleen called for the butler to come in.

"Forgive me," O'Connell entered. "But his lordship is on the phone and is asking for both Mr. O'Grady and Master Gregory."

Keelan and Viktor looked at each other, then, removing his napkin from his lap, Keelan wiped his mouth and stood.

"Please excuse us," he said to Kathleen.

"Tell him I'm upset he didn't want to speak with his mother too," Kathleen said winking at Viktor.

Chapter Six

As Jon and Courtney waited for Keelan and Viktor to answer the phone, Jon chuckled.

"My mother is going to be upset I didn't ask to speak with her too," Jon explained.

"Oh, you're gonna be in so much trouble," she teased.

"I'll get her some flowers," Jon shrugged.

"Hiya, Jon," they heard Keelan's voice on the other end of the phone. "Greg's with me."

"Hey, Keelan, I've got Courtney here with me, too. How are ya?" Jon replied.

"Grand grand, what's on your mind?" Keelan asked.

"Greg, how's everything going? You been able to see much of Ireland?" Jon dodged the question.

"We've done a lot of exploring here and in Cork, Mayo and

Galway. Once Iollan gets back from his trip with his girlfriend he promised to take me to Dublin and show me around," Viktor replied. "Oh, and your mom told me to tell you she's very upset with you that you didn't ask to speak with her too."

"Yeah, I know," Jon laughed. "I'm in trouble. But there was a very good reason. I'm calling on business."

"All right," Keelan replied. "What's going on?"

"I hate to bring this up especially now, Greg, but—"

"My father got off," Viktor finished. "I saw it on the internet. And he threatened you."

"Oh, you saw that, huh?" Jon asked.

"I've been following his trial for a while now," Viktor admitted.

"I'm sorry. I promised you a lot of things but I'm afraid they fell through," Jon apologized.

"And the two undercover cops? What happened to them?" Viktor asked. "They were supposed to testify, right?"

"They've disappeared," Courtney said.

"They're dead," Viktor replied. "Trust me."

"We suspected that," Jon sighed.

"Is there anything I can do?" Viktor asked.

"The best thing for you to do right now would be to lay low," Jon said. "But I wanted to pick your brain a little."

"Okay, shoot," Viktor offered.

"You don't need me for this and I'm sure Greg would speak more freely if I weren't here," Keelan said.

"No," Viktor replied. "Please stay, Keelan. What do you need to know?"

"Where would your father have dumped the bodies of the two cops?" Jon asked.

"One of the men who work for him is a plant supervisor at a waste plant south of Downtown. He normally utilizes the acres of land there. And the concrete trucks," Viktor explained.

"We were afraid of that," Jon sighed. "Listen, if I wanted to flip a member of your father's group, who would it be?"

Viktor thought a moment. "Probably Sergei," he said. "The one I was with when you got me out. He just had a kid and doesn't want her growing up like me. But he's also fiercely loyal and a close friend of my father. He knows where all the bodies are buried. But he's your best option for a turnover with knowledge. He always... had a soft spot for me. If you tell him I'm alive."

"No, not an option," Jon replied.

"But, Jon it could help. He knows the hell I went through. We got really close the last year," Viktor stopped speaking as if he revealed too much.

"Good to know," Jon went on without a pause. "But not an option. Also have you ever heard your father mention Judge Conner Cross?"

"The judge presiding over his case?" Viktor asked. "You think he was corrupt?"

"We're pursuing all lines of inquiry," Jon covered. "Had you heard of him before you left?"

"Honestly, no," Viktor said. "But it wasn't unusual for Father to have meetings behind closed doors without me. I'm probably not your best bet for information. I know some stuff but Father never mentioned his *clients* around me."

"All right, no worries," Jon replied. "Thanks, Greg. We'll call again when we have more information."

"Jon, Courtney, please be careful. He's not someone I want any of my friends messing with. He's ruthless," Viktor said.

"You have enough to worry about," Jon replied. "Don't worry about us. We'll be fine. Give my love to Ma and I'll talk to you both later."

As soon as Jon hung up the phone, Courtney logged into Jon's desktop computer with her credentials and ran a search on Conner Cross. "Hey, Jon, look at this. Looks like Cross was divorced many years ago, but he does have two daughters; Karen," she looked up at him. "And Donna."

"Daughter," Jon stated. "Can you get a number for her?"

"Give me a second," Courtney singed as she typed quickly on the keyboard. "Got it." Jon pulled out his phone while Courtney gave him the number listed.

"It's ringing." Jon said putting the phone to his ear. "Voicemail." Jon left a brief message with his name and number for her to call him back and hung up.

"You don't think she's going to call you back, do you?" Courtney asked.

"Doubtful," Jon answered just as his phone buzzed twice in

his hand. "Kim." He stated when Courtney's eyebrows rose. Tapping out a text to her, he sent it and walked to the front door.

"How is he?" Kim asked as soon as she cleared the threshold.

"He's shaken," Jon answered. Turning the corner, Kim saw Courtney and rushed to hug her friend.

"How are you?" she asked.

"Back at it," Courtney admitted. "Doing great."

Scott trotted down the front stairs wearing Northwestern University sweat pants and a white t-shirt.

"Hey baby," he crooned saddling up to her and dropping his arm around her waist. "Thanks for coming."

"You know I would've been here in a heartbeat if I could've," she said kissing him gently.

"I know," he answered. "Let's go downstairs and let Dad and Courtney be."

"Before you go, Kim," Jon called her back. "Did you ever work with Judge Connor Cross?"

"Once or twice," she replied. "He was tough but fair. Are you wondering if he was crooked?"

"Exploring all avenues, Counselor," Jon answered. "But nothing odd with his work that you saw?"

"Nothing," she said.

"If you think of anything," Jon prompted.

"I'll think about it, but nothing comes to mind," Kim shrugged and walked with Scott down the stairs to the basement.

Once they were alone, Courtney looked around the room. "Where's Beth?" she asked.

"At her office getting ahead of the deadline," Jon replied. "Her editor is hounding her."

"Well, with the wedding to plan and the book to write it's a wonder she's still sane, especially saying yes to you," Courtney teased.

"Oh, now I know you're feeling better," Jon answered. Then after a moment of silence, he walked around to the printer behind his desk and pulled out several sheets of computer paper. "Okay, so all we know currently," Jon said scrawling a few notes on the papers. "Is that Cross was killed after letting a well-known mobster with an iron clad case walk out of the courtroom. His last words were, they have his daughter and forced him to let Redorvsky off. Can you run a background on Cross and get his phone records? I want to see the last numbers both that he called and that called him?"

"On it," Courtney turned back to the computer and started typing.

"I'm going to—" Jon was cut off by the doorbell ringing. Motioning Courtney to wait and be quiet, Jon went to the door. "Yeah, who is it?"

"John Ireland with Ireland and Sons Plumbing," a familiar voice called out. "We were called about a leak in the kitchen."

Courtney and Jon locked eyes.

"Oh, yeah one second," Jon called back and unlatched the door. Steven stood before them in a plumber's uniform, gear and baseball cap. "Thanks for coming on such short notice."

"Not a problem," Steven answered. "Where's the leak?"

"This way," Jon replied and as soon as he shut the door behind him, Steven signaled him to be quiet.

"You have a great house," Steven said. Courtney's brow furrowed.

"You're not the usual guy who comes out," Jon answered.

"Nah that's Billy," Steven replied. "He's out."

The mention of his old Vietnam War friend and the man who was shot and killed by Riley a couple months ago gave Jon pause.

"Yeah, I wondered," he finally continued. "Follow me to the kitchen, let me show you the leak. I have a towel tied around it."

"That's a great idea," Steven pulled out a small square box and raised the antenna. "Oh yep, I see it. Let's see what we're dealing with here." Flipping a switch on the box, Steven waited for a moment, tapped his ear where Courtney, from her angle, could see an ear bud. Then he stepped closer to Jon. "Okay, that'll dampen our voices and play a prerecorded track," Steven spoke quietly. "I've only got a couple minutes. Listen, Jon you have to stay away from the Redorvsky case."

"Why?" Jon asked.

"I can't go into detail, but you both need to steer clear, okay?" Steven said.

"Steven, you have to give us more than that," Jon replied.

"Bury it," Steven ordered. "You have to."

"Redorvsky was our collar," Jon stated.

"He's part of a bigger plan here, Jon, listen to me," Steven stepped closer. "If I could tell you, I would, but I can't without compromising things that have taken years to plan."

"And Cross?" Courtney asked.

"He's collateral," Steven replied. Then looking at her shocked face, he continued. "As callous as that sounds, that's what it has to be."

"Until you catch Redorvsky and he takes a plea bargain. Cross and everyone that man has killed will have no justice," Courtney said.

"*Justice* is not my business," Steven answered.

"No, it's ours," Jon replied. "And I'm with Courtney on this, Steven."

"Listen to me, for god's sake," Steven whispered harshly. "I *will* shut you down if I have to but I wanted to come to you first as family. Let it go."

"Family or not, we can't do that," Jon replied. "There's more to Cross's death than just a master plan to get Redorvsky."

"It's not just Redorvsky, Jon," Steven said. "This plan goes far above your clearance but I have agents in the field *who will die* if you continue this ridiculous pursuit."

"Ridiculous?" Courtney asked. "Asking us to stop doing our jobs is like us asking you to stop sleeping with women to get intel."

"Courtney," Jon stopped her. "Maybe we should listen to him."

"You can't be serious," Courtney replied shadows of their conversation last month where Jon took Steven over her, reared its head. Jon locked eyes with her and slowly she nodded. "Okay, fine. We'll drop it. But you get the heat from Dave when we tell him, Steven."

"I will deal with the captain," Steven answered. "But for now, just promise me you will stop looking into Connor Cross."

"Promise," Jon replied. "But I expect an answer when all this is over."

"And you will get one," Steven promised. "I need you to trust me."

Jon looked back at his partner who nodded, then turned to Steven.

"We do," Jon answered.

"Good, now I need to go," Steven paused a moment then switched the square box off. "That outta do it, sir. Nothing a good tweak couldn't fix."

"Thank you so much for your help," Jon said. "We look forward to using you again in the future should the need arise."

Steven paused a moment before he opened the door and looked back at Jon, his eyes were hard. *I mean it, Jon,* he mouthed before he opened the door and headed back to his van.

"You aren't seriously going to stop our investigation, are you?" Courtney asked as soon as Jon walked back into the study.

"Into Connor Cross?" Jon clarified. "Yes." Holding up his hand when she started to protest. "Into *Donna* Cross? Hell no." A grin slid across Courtney's lips.

"You old devil," she laughed.

"Old?" he teased. "So tell me, Partner do we have an address for Ms. Donna Cross?"

"Did he listen to you? Is he going to drop it?" Brent asked as Steven opened the door to the loft.

"What do you think?" Steven demanded. "Jon is a stubborn bastard sometimes."

"Like father like son," Brent laughed.

"Shut up," Steven replied. "You're going to have to tail them for both of us now. Has she made contact?"

"I have a text from Meredith telling me to follow them but that's it right now," Brent replied.

"We need to find out why she wants them followed," Steven replied. After a moment, Steven turned back to Brent. "How are we with O'Malley?"

"Zoe's in Minneapolis and made contact," Brent replied. "With some help from our resident Irishman."

"Keep me posted on what Meredith wants and get some sleep. I doubt they'll head out until the early hours. I'll take over."

"Sure thing, boss," he replied and slid out of the chair heading to the bedroom and closing the door.

"Jesus, Jon what the hell have you gotten yourself into?" Steven breathed.

Chapter Seven

"Thank you, sir," Jon stated over the phone and hung up.

Looking over at Courtney, he walked back into the study. "The Mayor is glad to assist in our investigation."

"Good, you never did tell me how you know him. Golfing buddies?" Courtney asked.

"Chess club actually," Jon replied. "I, of course, let him win… occasionally."

"I bet you do," Courtney laughed. "What did he say?"

"He calls Cross a *state treasure* and his death a *national tragedy*," Jon answered. "Golfing buddies, I guess."

"I guess," Courtney said. "He doesn't think he could be crooked?"

"No, as he said it, 'Connor upheld the law with absolute rigor. He wouldn't let anyone off even if they held his grandmother at knife point.' Also a little interesting tidbit he let me in on, Cross was on the shortlist for State Supreme Court Justice."

"Redorvsky could have used an Indiana Court Justice. Why kill him?"

"It wasn't guaranteed but from what the mayor told me he wasn't one to shirk responsibility. Maybe they knew he wouldn't keep quiet after he got his daughter back."

"True," Courtney nodded.

"But he did say he'll back us if we have any issue with any of the acronyms," Jon replied.

"NSA, FBI, CIA," Courtney rattled off.

"Exactly," Jon answered. "Have the phone records come back yet?"

"Not yet," she answered. "But his background has. He's clean, Jon. One traffic ticket back in '74 but other than that, nothing."

"What about the two daughters?" Jon asked.

"Both live in Minneapolis," she replied.

"Hmm… you wanna know what I'm thinking?" Jon said.

"Pizza and a beer?" She offered.

"That's scary," Jon teased. "Besides that, I'm thinking road trip."

"All because she didn't answer her phone?" Courtney asked.

"That, and also I don't want to be around when Steven finds out we aren't following his advice."

"Advice?" Courtney said. "You mean order?"

"Suggestion… strong suggestion," Jon amended.

"Phone records," Courtney called leaning forward when the computer dinged. "Last call was to a burner phone. I have the number but little good it would do."

"Do we want to go under the impression that this was Redorvsky?" Jon asked.

"Well, hear me out on this," Courtney turned in the chair and faced him. "Steven said there are more things about this case than Redorvsky. What if it's someone else?"

"I was thinking that too," Jon asked.

"Maybe like another mob boss?" she replied.

"Possibly," Jon said. "I'm going to call the other sister, Karen was it? And see if she answers. If not, I want to go there. Minnesota isn't too far. We could make it in a few hours."

"I don't know if I can get away right now," Courtney said.

"You have another job you haven't told me about?" Jon asked.

"Yeah, actually, that of future wife and wedding planner," she answered.

"Courtney, this is your job. This is what you are here to do. You can't expect us not to follow the leads when they present themselves."

"When have I ever done that, Jon?" she stood and crossed her arms. "I think I've shown I'm pretty damned loyal."

"The facts tell us we need to go."

"The facts tell us there are no facts. We have no evidence."

"Exactly the reason we need to go."

"Is this some kind of measuring contest between you and Steven?"

"No, of course not. This is where the facts are pointing. We must follow up."

"Jesus, fine," she threw her hands up and sighed.

"Good, be back here tomorrow morning around five," Jon said. "We'll probably be gone a couple days."

"Then I'm heading out now to spend time with my fiancé," she said gathering her things. "Goodnight."

"No need to be upset with me," Jon replied. "I'm simply saying what needs to be done."

"What *needs* to be done? Or what should be done?"

"They're not the same thing."

"Getting that," she answered. "At least not with you."

"What is your problem?"

"My problem? Oh, I don't know, Jon maybe it's because it's my first day back and my partner can't wait to tell me what to do again especially when it comes to *Steven*. I thought you learned something from *last* time."

"This has nothing to do with that and you throw an old sin in my face?"

"Old sins cast long shadows isn't that the saying?" She demanded.

"You think I'm telling you something no one else would say? Trust me, Courtney you couldn't handle some of the partners on the force. I am not ordering you. I am reminding you what needs to be done."

"Clearly," she went to the door. "I'll be here at five."

Chapter Eight

Courtney slammed the door to her apartment and stalked up the stairs. Ryan walked out of the kitchen to greet her, but paused at the top of the stairs when he saw her face. He turned back to the fridge, pulled out the bottle of white wine and a glass from the hooks under the cabinets. Opening the wine bottle, he poured a large glass and took it to her as she stripped out of her suit pants and blouse in the bedroom.

"Here," he said offering her the glass. Accepting it from him, she downed half of it in one go.

"Your uncle," was all she said before taking another large gulp.

"I figured," he answered. "Come." Leading her into the bathroom, he ran a bath for her, and helped her out of her remaining clothes. As soon as she sank deep into the bubbles, Ryan kissed her forehead and whispered, "I'll be right back." She nodded and took the wine glass from him, watching him leave the room. He had flipped off the glaring florescent lights and turned on the ambient lamp she kept in the corner of the counter. Closing her eyes, she laid her head back onto the bath pillow he had set behind her head and took a deep breath. A couple minutes later, Ryan came back into the room carrying a wine bucket filled with ice containing the bottle of white wine and his glass. Setting his glass on the counter and the bucket on the toilet seat, he lit her lavender aromatherapy candle and stripped out of his t-shirt and jeans then stepped into the tub opposite her.

He didn't say anything only took a drink of his wine and set it on the floor beside him. Pulling one of her legs up out of the water, he began to softly massage her foot. Groaning, she looked at him.

"You're amazing," she said.

"Shh," he replied softly and she heard soft classic rock and jazz ballads, Ryan's favorite music playing softly from the other room. Simon and Garfunkel sang about the sound of silence and rosemary and thyme, followed by Frank Sinatra's ballad about flying to the moon and witchcraft. Once Paul McCartney started singing about live and let die, Courtney was well and truly relaxed and pruny.

Looking at her fiancé as he poured more wine into her glass finishing off the bottle, she pulled up and straddled his lap. Threading her fingers through his hair, she leaned into him and kissed him softly.

"You are absolutely the most amazing man I've ever met," she said. His boyish grin sent a pang of need straight to her core.

"Wanna talk about what happened?" he asked.

"That's not exactly what I want to do right now," she answered.

"Oh, I know," he teased. "But I first want to know what happened."

She leaned back in the tub and sighed. Taking a swallow of her wine, she played with the bubbles.

"I jumped," she replied. "He didn't mean anything by it but I took it wrong and rubber banded back to when he chose Steven over me."

"Steven's involved?" Ryan asked. She nodded and he continued. "What happened?"

"This case has ties in Minneapolis and we're going to have to follow up and go there tonight."

"How does Steven fit in?"

"He's warned us to stay away, something to do with a case he's working on to take Redorvsky down."

"And you're not listening to him?" Ryan asked calmly taking a drink.

"Judge Cross was killed in broad daylight. That's my job to solve. He isn't my boss, he doesn't get to tell me what cases to do or not."

"No, but he is a special agent with one of the most powerful intelligence agencies in the world. If he says to stay away, then shouldn't you?"

"No, Jon and I need to follow these leads and go where the facts are telling us to go and they're saying Minneapolis."

Ryan smirked and raised his glass to his lips. "That sounds a lot like something Uncle Jon would say."

"Sometimes I hate you," she narrowed her eyes at him.

"No, you don't," he drank from his glass but didn't break eye contact with her. "So, you need to go to Minneapolis tonight, what time?"

"Jon wants me at his house at five in the morning," she explained.

"We have about twelve hours... oh, there's so much I can do to you in twelve hours," his eyes danced as he reached out, sloshing water over the sides of the tub to grab her and tickle her around the waist before locking his lips with hers in a long passionate kiss.

"Why do I get the shitty schedule?" Brent Tyler asked sitting outside Jon's house at four-thirty in the morning.

"Just think of it this way, you get to go on vacation," he heard Steven's voice in his ear.

"And do I tell Meredith?" Brent asked.

"You know what to do," he answered. "We need information. Let her use you."

"You know, I usually like to be used by a woman, but this..."

his voice trailed off.

"Just keep your head in the game, Tyler," Steven said. "We need this to work."

"Aye aye, Captain," he teased. "Oops, heads up," he leaned forward and took his binoculars off the dashboard. "Looks like Courtney showed up after all."

"Go dark, check in when you can," Steven ordered.

"Got it," he answered and pulled out his ear bud, rolled the window down and tossed it out. Opening his glove compartment, he pulled out another phone and checked in. "I'm here," he said. "Greene and Shields are heading out. Do you know where they're going?"

"My guess would be Minneapolis," Meredith said. "I'm already here. Follow them and let me know when they get to town. Do not let them notice they have a tail."

"I have done this before," he answered.

"You're a petty criminal, Brent," she replied. "Don't try and make it out like you're some badass from a Die Hard movie."

Brent clenched his teeth. "I've got it handled," he replied.

"Good, we'll be waiting for you," she answered and clicked off.

———————◦◦◦———————

"I'm glad you came," Jon said as he and Courtney waited at a light. "I'm sorry I was so callous earlier."

"No, Jon, I jumped. I'm sorry," Courtney answered. "I

should never have rubber banded. I guess I'm still not over what happened."

"You have no idea how much I hate what I said to you that day," he said. "You did not deserve any of it. I was too blinded with the desire to show Steven he was my son, I lost focus on what was important. If you hadn't gotten out of that warehouse, I don't think I would have ever forgiven myself."

"You can't say that," Courtney countered. "We both made our choices and I chose to follow Rob without any backup. Don't beat yourself up. I'm just not over everything and sometimes I lash out and other times I freeze. Ryan has been amazing helping me work through it but he's not here."

"I know," Jon said. "I've been there. Mat had a horrible case of PTSD when we returned from 'Nam. I should have seen the signs and not ordered you."

"No, I need things to be the same between us," she answered. "Really, it's okay. Thank you for your apology and I hope you accept mine."

"Do you even have to ask?" Jon smiled. "I'm so glad you have Ryan."

"Me too," her lovesick sigh made Jon laugh.

"Gross," he teased breaking the mood.

"I'm starving, wanna stop somewhere?"

"Already ahead of you," Jon replied pulling into a fast food restaurant as Courtney picked a playlist on her iPod.

Chapter Nine

Courtney woke from a doze as Jon pulled into a gas station. She stretched her neck relieving the kinks from a couple hours' sleep in a car. Looking over at Jon, she straightened and looked around.

"Where are we?" she asked, her voice rough with sleep.

"On the boarder of Illinois and Minnesota," Jon said turning off the car and pulling out his wallet. "Just getting some gas, need a break?"

"Yeah, I'm gonna run in," she replied, grabbing her purse. "Want anything?"

"I'll be in in a minute," Jon answered stepping out and walking around the car. Courtney stepped into the gas station and found the restroom. After washing her hands, she saw Jon enter, heading to the men's room. Going up and down the aisles grabbing some snacks, not watching where she was going, Courtney ran straight into a man with dark brown hair and the snacks she had picked out went flying.

"Oh, I am so sorry," Courtney said. "I wasn't looking."

"No no, my fault, I shouldn't have been looking at my phone," he replied bending down to help her. "You live around here? Or just passing through?"

"On our way to the twin cities," she answered.

"Fun," he answered. "I grew up around there. What brings you to town?"

"Courtney?" Jon's voice came from behind her and she turned.

"Hey... baby," she said. Jon's eyes twitched imperceptibly.

"You ready?" he asked.

"Yeah," she answered. "Babe, this is... I'm sorry I didn't catch your name."

"Tyler, Brent Tyler," he said.

"Brent," she stated. "We kinda ran into each other."

"Nice to meet you," Jon replied.

"Likewise," he answered.

"Ready? We should get back on the road," Jon said.

"Yep," Courtney answered removing a speck of invisible lent off his shoulder and smiling at him, then turned back to Brent. "Thanks so much for your help and again I'm sorry."

"No worries," he stated. "No harm done."

Once Jon grabbed a couple snacks, he paid and they both

went back to his car. Safely inside, he turned to her.

"Who was that guy?" he asked.

"I don't know," she answered. "But... I've seen him before somewhere. We randomly bumped into each other here. Or I should say he bumped into me."

"You know him how?" Jon asked.

"I can't place it, but it's not recent," she replied.

"He was trying to do something with your purse or I wouldn't have said anything."

"What do you mean?" she pulled up her handbag and looked through it.

"Not sure, but I saw his hand move toward it when you weren't looking," he said. "Wanna call Dave and have him get the security feed?" Jon asked.

"Maybe, let's wait just around the corner to see if he follows and what kind of car he drives, then I'll call. Could just be a petty criminal."

"Good idea," Jon answered.

Steven's phone rang as he spoke with Danny. Recognizing the ringtone, he excused himself and answered.

"Hey," he said.

"Hey, baby," Amber stated. "I know you're working but I needed to call you."

"Everything okay?" Steven asked.

"It's Josh," she sighed. "He's missing you and taking it out on me. Could you talk to him? I'm at my wit's end."

Steven chuckled. "Put him on," he said.

"Thank you," she breathed.

Steven waited until he heard his future step-son's voice.

"Josh, what's going on?" Steven asked.

"Mom's being mean," he whined.

"Tell me why you think that."

"Because she is," he complained.

"Joshua," Steven stated.

"I only asked for something else for dinner," he said.

"*After* you were sitting down? And *after* you said you didn't want to eat what she made?"

"It was fish, I don't like fish, she knows this," he tried to justify.

"You love fish, don't give me that," he said. "You love it when I make it."

"That's different," he said.

"Josh, you can't do this to your mom right now, okay?"

"Why? She's being mean."

"Joshua, that's enough. She needs you to be the man of the house while I'm not there, okay?"

"When are you going to be home?"

"I'm not sure, Buddy," Steven answered. "But soon. I promise. I need you to take care of your mom. Promise me."

"Okay," he sulked.

"Thank you, big man. I love you, buddy, put your mom back on for me," he said. When Amber came back on the line, he continued. "How are you feeling?"

"Okay," she answered. "Still sick in the mornings."

"I'm sorry," he said.

"You should be," she teased. "It's all your fault."

"My fault? As I remember you were a willing participant."

"*Very* willing," she agreed. "But I'm fine, baby. I want you home. I worry about you, but I know you're doing what you were called to do. Just please be careful. Your family can't be without you."

"I swear to you, I am being careful," he promised. "And I'm going to be home very soon, okay?"

"Okay," she said. "I love you."

"I love you, Amber. I'll call when I get to the hotel tonight, okay?"

"Give 'em hell, Casanova," she stated.

"I intend to," he answered.

Steven hung up and tapped the phone on his hand, sighing. He loved and hated the feelings stirring within him. They had yet to tell his mother or Jon their news but he needed to get through the mission before he thought about his future. Turning back to Danny, he apologized for the interruption.

"The wife?" Danny asked.

"Almost."

"How far along is she?" Danny asked. Steven looked up sharply. "Sorry, I couldn't help but overhear. Congratulations."

"Thank you, and she's about eight weeks," he said. "We haven't told our parents yet."

"Nah, I understand," he answered.

"You have kids?" Steven asked, though knew the answer from his file. Danny didn't answer immediately and his face went stoic.

"Did," he said. "Now, let's get back to this."

"Right," Steven let the subject drop and focused on instructing Danny on his next mission.

Chapter Ten

Courtney and Jon pulled into Minneapolis at four o'clock. Their meeting with the Police Chief was scheduled at six giving just enough time to check into their hotel, relax, shower and change.

Jon had requested adjoining rooms and Courtney immediately unlocked her side, knocking on Jon's. He opened it and she leaned against the door frame watching him hang up his garment bag in the closet.

"I'm going to shower," she said. "What time are we meeting the chief?"

"Dinner reservations are at six," Jon explained pulling out his phone and confirming the details in the email. "It's walking distance from where we are. We should probably be out the door by quarter 'til."

"Does it give a dress code?"

"No, but I'm just going with business professional without the tie," he answered.

"Got it," she replied.

"Knock on the door when you're out of the shower. Keep it ajar, I won't come in."

"I know you won't," she replied. "And I will."

Brent pulled to a stop outside the five-star hotel Jon and Courtney were staying at in downtown Minneapolis. He parked his van and texted Meredith to let her know where he was. Bumping into Courtney at the gas station was not planned but he needed to slip the note into her handbag. Unfortunately, Jon interrupted them when he caught him reaching for it. His phone buzzed in the cup holder, a text from Meredith telling him to get a room for the night and to check his checking account.

Checking his bank account, the first installment of Meredith's blood money had hit.

Heading in now, he texted back.

"Courtney," Jon called as he pulled his shirt cuffs through his blazer sleeve. "We should get going."

She had knocked on the door when she got out of the shower about forty-five minutes ago but since then he hadn't heard anything. He walked over to the door and knocked.

"Courtney?" He waited.

"I'm almost ready," she called back. "Thirty seconds."

"No worries," he answered checking his watch. Turning back into his suite he took his phone and pocketed it. Hearing the door open, he turned. "Wow," he smiled.

"Ready," she smiled.

"You look great but are you going to be able to walk in those?" He indicated her ankle strapped stilettos.

"Oh yeah," she replied. "They're my most comfortable pair of shoes."

"I like them," he said offering her to go ahead of him and out to the hallway.

"So give me the run down," she said.

"Chief Pellegrino is young, early forties and ambitious. We're also meeting with Kyle Harris the PR director and younger than the chief. By all accounts, he's a bit of a player. So..."

"Use my feminine charm to get answers?" she laughed.

"If you feel comfortable," he said.

"I'm a cop," she answered. "I make myself comfortable."

"Come on, I looked up the restaurant menu online, they have an excellent wine list and they are known for their ahi tuna and sushi appetizer."

"That sounds like my kind of place," she replied as the elevator doors closed.

⸻⸻◦⸻⸻

Brent looked out from his hiding place at the opposite end

of the hallway when he heard the elevator doors close. Walking to Jon's door, he looked both ways before using the key card he had stolen off a hotel housekeeper. Having already looped the security feed, he breathed a sigh of relief when no one came out of the other rooms.

Once inside, his eyes darted around the room. Donning his latex gloves, he headed toward the adjoining doors, still open and looked for a place to put the device he had in his pocket. His eyes rested on the lamp bolted to the desk up against the wall. Sliding the device between the bolted holder and the wall, he tested it. When it worked, he pulled out his phone and sent a text.

Done, was all it said. As he walked out of the room, he quickly erased the text and restored the phone to factory settings tossing it into the fake plant when he walked down the hallway.

Pulling out his secondary phone, the one from the glove compartment, he sent a text to Meredith.

Brent: Couldn't get into the rooms. Room numbers 805 and 807. Will need Zach to plant bug.

He waited for a response and pushed the elevator button.

Meredith: Understood, but do not appreciate this lack of capability.

Suppressing a chuckle, he shook his head and entered the elevator car when the doors opened.

Chapter Eleven

Jon and Courtney walked the two blocks to the restaurant enjoying downtown and the beautifully clear evening. Finding the restaurant, they went in and gave their names. Immediately, escorted to a back table, they saw two men seated, one in his early forties and the other, early to mid-thirties. The older man stood and smiled at them, extending his hand first to Jon then to Courtney.

"Lieutenant Greene and Detective Shields, I presume," he smiled. "Adam Pellegrino. Welcome to the twin cities. Please sit."

"Thank you," Jon replied holding Courtney's chair for her, then sitting next to her. "It's very nice of you to meet with us outside of the precinct, Chief."

"Oh, no need for all of that. I'm a bit unconventional," he grinned. "I like to meet our visiting brothers and sisters in blue in a laid-back atmosphere. Allow me to introduce my Media Relations and PR Director Kyle Harris," the chief said. The man beside him smiled.

"Pleasure," Jon said.

"I hope you don't find this offensive but I have taken the liberty of ordering a bottle of wine for us," the chief replied.

"Not at all," Jon replied opening the menu.

"And may I recommend the sushi," he smiled. "It is some of the best in town."

"We are both fans of Sushi," Jon replied.

"Big fans," Courtney replied. "But I'm also looking at this grilled chicken balsamic."

"That is also very good, Detective," the chief said.

"Oh please, Chief, when I'm out of uniform, it's Courtney," she said moving her left hand down to her lap and discretely taking off her engagement ring. Jon's hand lay palm open on his thigh and she slipped her ring onto it. He pocketed it by pretending to shift his wallet in his back pocket.

"Adam then," the chief replied.

"And Kyle," the PR director winked. Courtney smiled flirtatiously back at him. "I was curious, Lieutenant," Kyle Harris went on looking over at Jon. "Why do you believe Donna Cross's death is so important?"

Jon and Courtney looked at each other, shock evident on their faces.

"Death?" Jon asked looking back at Kyle. "Donna Cross is dead?"

"Found on the steps of the courthouse yesterday morning," Adam explained. "I'm sorry I thought you knew, that's why you are here. She was killed the same day as her father in Indianapolis."

"We hadn't heard," Courtney stated. "How was she killed?"

"Execution style, two in the back of the head," Adam explained.

"Does she have any family in the area?" Jon asked.

"We've been trying to get a hold of her sister Karen but there's been no answer at her house or over the phone," Adam said.

"Could you tell us what happened back in Indianapolis?" Kyle asked. "Maybe a little *quid pro quo*?"

"Of course," Jon said. "Connor Cross was a judge back in Indy. He was presiding over a very volatile case involving the Russian mob. We believe they are involved in her death."

"Meaning they could have used his daughter against him," the chief summed up. Jon nodded. "Was the judgement thrown out?"

"It will be if we can get the evidence we need. If we can prove Judge Cross was compromised, we can have the case retried." Jon explained.

"MPD is at your disposal. Anything you need, just let us know," the chief said. "I'll get you the names of the detectives in charge and give them explicit instructions to work with you."

"Thank you," Jon replied. "We appreciate it."

They stopped when the waiter came back with the bottle of wine and took their orders. After they toasted and drank, Adam

Pellegrino spoke again.

"I know this is a business meeting but I just can't bring myself to talk business when I'm drinking a good glass of wine and looking at a beautiful woman." His eyes locked on Courtney.

"I completely understand that," Jon answered raising his glass and winking at her.

"How long have you two been partners?" Kyle asked.

"Oh god," Jon chuckled leaning back.

"About three years," Courtney answered.

"A very fast three years," Jon smiled.

"I was a rookie when I was partnered to him and he has taught me everything I know," Courtney explained.

"Well, not everything," he replied. "She was top of her class."

"He's been a great partner," Courtney said taking his hand.

"It's been an adventure," Jon replied. "But I couldn't imagine having a better partner."

"Tell us a little about yourselves," Adam asked.

Jon and Courtney left the restaurant after dinner. The sun had set and the street lights were on; the hustle and bustle of the city surrounded them. Jon handed over her engagement ring and Courtney slipped it back on as she looked down the street.

"Hmm, it's so pretty," Courtney said.

"It's still early, do you want to walk around?" Jon asked.

"I would," she said. "I also hear Irish music."

"So do I, it's called *Wild Rover*," he answered. "Wanna go?"

"Definitely," she replied taking his arm. Down the road about three blocks, was an Irish pub with a live band playing. Jon paid the cover and Courtney found one seat at the bar. Jon stood at the bar next to her, leaning down when he saw Courtney say something but couldn't hear her.

"I don't really want anything to drink," she said. "Sorry you had to pay the cover."

He shook his head and patted her hand.

"No worries," he called back. "But I'm having a dessert drink."

"What are you getting?" she asked.

"I'm thinking Baileys," he said.

"That does sounds good," she answered.

Waving the bartender over Jon ordered their drinks over the din of the music. Listening to the song, Jon started when he felt Courtney grip his arm. His eyes shot over to hers and he leaned in.

"Look at the front door," she said loudly enough for him to hear but not loud enough for anyone else. Jon nodded then nonchalantly turned and looked around. His eyes landed on two men walking in. One, he had never seen before, but the other was the same man who had run into Courtney at the gas station. The bartender brought their drinks and Jon turned back to accept it and asked for the check.

"Interesting," Jon replied. "Sláinte," he toasted, clinking his glass with hers. "Drink up, let's see if they follow us when we leave."

"No, I have a better idea," she said. "Go with me on this."

"I'm not going to like this, am I?" he asked accepting the check and pulling out a twenty-dollar bill.

"Probably not," she replied tipping her drink back and giving a shout. The band started a rock and roll song and she swayed to it. Once the music picked up, she cheered and stood dancing to the music as if she were drunk. Grabbing Jon's hand, she swiveled him around and begged him to dance with her. After a couple feigned attempts to put her off, he agreed and went with her to the make shift dance floor. Courtney turned her back to his front and pushed her body closer, grinding against him. Jon's hands landed on her hips as he swayed with her.

After the song, Jon grabbed her hand and tugged her outside. They hailed a taxi and still pretended to be intoxicated as they climbed in. The two men they had seen enter earlier followed them out but once Jon told the driver where to go, they disappeared around a corner.

"Not too terrible, right?" Courtney asked shaking her hair free of the up do.

"No, thankfully," he replied. "Let's stay alert though see if they follow us."

Chapter Twelve

Agent Zoe Christie lay in Liam O'Malley's arms stroking the light hair on his chest.

"That was fun," she said.

"Yeah," he breathed.

"You really know how to treat a girl," she leaned up to look at him. "Are all Irishmen that skilled?"

"Just me," he grinned.

"Oh, come on," she laughed.

"I'm serious," he replied. "I bet no man has ever taken care of you like I have."

"True," she bit her lip. "But I think you might have to prove it again."

"Insatiable?" he chuckled.

"Hey, I'm a grown woman, I know what I want," she

answered. "Besides my ex-boyfriend never could keep me satisfied."

"Gay?" he asked.

"Don't think so," she replied. "He's just a lot older and I mean a lot."

"You were screwing grandpa? No wonder you're insatiable," he went on and turned her on her back.

"Think you can keep up?" she asked pushing him onto his back and taking her place above him.

"I think it's worth a try," he replied grabbing her hips. Just as he leaned up to kiss her, the door burst open and an older man walked in. "Da'!" Liam cried covering them both before his father saw more of his son than he wanted. "What the hell are ye doing?"

"I could ask you the same thing," the father said. "What do you think you're doing bringing a girl back here? I've told you if you can't keep it in your pants then go somewhere no one will know."

"It's not like that, Da', Katie is—"

"Oh, she's a Katie, is she?" his eyes danced to Zoe's face though he kept talking to his son. "Do you honestly think that red hair is real? You're an eejit, Liam."

"Hey," Zoe yelled sitting up, revealing her naked body to both sets of hungry eyes. "I don't know who the hell you think you are, old man but Liam is showing me a good time and if you have a problem with that or me you can just take your Guinness belly out of here and downstairs. I can hear the music from here. I'm guessing you're having some sort of party in your precious little bar downstairs. Let the younger O'Malley satisfy a woman since it's clear you haven't satisfied anyone for a long time," Zoe knew it was a dangerous line she just crossed and O'Malley Senior, her true mark, could easily toss her out or worse, but from what Danny had told her, the old man liked fire.

Both men stared at her and Senior blinked a few times.

"What's your name, *cailín?*" Senior asked.

"Kathleen Dunne and before you ask, no my red hair isn't real because even though my family may be, generations back, Irish, that gene failed to be passed to me so instead of wallowing in self-pity which isn't my style, I got it done. Happy now, jackass?"

Senior's eyes caressed her skin from head to thigh since she was standing beside the bed.

"Eammon O'Malley, it's a pleasure," he said.

"It would have been had you not interrupted," she cocked her head to the side. "Your son is quite skilled."

"He learned from the best," the arrogance in his voice made her roll her eyes.

"Yeah okay sure, old man," she said.

"Be careful, girl," he replied. "You don't know who you're speaking to."

"Oh? I would have thought that was obvious," she answered. "You're a sex starved old man who can't bear to have a son better looking and better in bed than he is. But you know, it's okay. I never did mind an audience."

"Want to see who's better?" he asked.

"Da', she's mine," Liam whined.

"Shut up, lad," Eammon's eyes never left hers.

After the appropriate wait time, Zoe shrugged. He was playing right into her hands. "Why not? I'm already hot and bothered and in need. Since your intrusion has left your son unprepared to deal with it, I'll take it where I can."

Eammon offered his hand. Zoe walked around the bed and took it.

"Come on, Katie," Liam whined. "It won't take me long."

"Too late, lad," she mimicked Eammon. "You've lost out to age and experience."

The smirk on Eammon's face as she took his hand and wrapped his coat around her shoulders made her smile, but for a completely different reason.

Gotcha, she thought.

———

"What did you think of Chief Pellegrino?" Jon asked as he and Courtney strolled into the hotel lobby after the taxi dropped them off.

"He's very young," she answered.

"Yes, he is," Jon agreed.

"And a bit too sure of himself," she went on.

"Agreed," Jon said.

"What did you feel about him?" She asked.

"He's a bit unorthodox and of course my initial reaction is to mistrust everyone but I didn't see anything particularly wrong with him but it's clear he's going to be watching us very closely."

The elevator doors opened and they stepped out onto their floor.

"Now I'm not so sure about Kyle Harris," Courtney said. "I haven't made up my—"

She was cut off by Jon grabbing her arm, pushing her into a darkened alcove and pressing his lips to hers. Stunned, she didn't move at first, but when he moaned against her mouth, she tentatively wrapped her arms around his neck and kissed him back. Knowing there was a reason for his sudden, odd, behavior, she played along. However, when he grabbed her leg and wrapped it around his hip, pushing the hem of her dress scandalously high, she pushed on his chest. He was crossing a major line.

Finally, Jon pulled back and locked eyes with her.

"I'm sorry," he whispered.

"What the hell did you see, Jon?" she demanded. Blowing out a breath that moved her hair, Jon motioned his head to the elevator. She looked up at the numbers to see it going down to the next level.

"Someone coming out of my room and I didn't want them to know I saw him," he said.

"Who was it?" she asked.

"Not sure but I could have sworn I saw a glint of a badge and a sidearm," he revealed.

"A cop?" she asked. "Do you think Pellegrino had us tailed already?"

"I didn't want to risk it," Jon whispered. "Maybe he saw us, maybe he didn't, but if he did and he is working for Pellegrino, he'll tell him we're sleeping together and that might help you a little in the investigation."

"Because he'll think I'm easy?"

"Give me a little more credit than that, okay?" Jon replied. "If he thinks we're sleeping together then he has something to hold over us. No fraternization, remember? It could be the leverage he needs and when he's cocky enough to think he's got us, he might reveal something damning."

"Okay," she wrapped her arms around her and looked over Jon's shoulder. "Can I get out of this alcove, now?"

"Hey, come on," Jon said. "It was necessary."

She nodded but didn't say anything. Jon huffed a sigh and stepped aside. She walked to her door and without looking back at him, unlocked it and let the door close behind her.

"Did you plant it?" The man asked. Zachary nodded. "Did he see you?"

"He was too busy making out with his partner," Zachary replied.

"Interesting," the man started. "Are you sure you weren't seen?"

"Not entirely, but I'm pretty sure," Zach shrugged.

"Pretty sure doesn't work for me," the man pulled out his

gun and fired. A stunned Zachary looked back at him as blood trickled down his forehead and he fell forward. "God, it's hard to find good people these days. In my father's time, people knew what was expected of them."

Meredith stepped out of the darkness.

"Look at you, Mr. Big-Bad-Mob-Boss. Tell me, what it felt like? Tell me you liked it."

"Come over here and I'll show you how much I liked it," he said.

Chapter Thirteen

Courtney paced her hotel room. Jon's kiss didn't bother her as much as his words did. She may have put up a good front earlier when she said she would make herself comfortable with whatever she had to do, but truthfully, she was scared. It wasn't who she was. She felt dirty just thinking about playing Adam and Kyle.

It hadn't been twenty-four hours since she had last seen Ryan and now all she wanted to do was to curl up with him. Fear of his reaction stopped her from calling him but she desperately needed to hear his voice. The walls around her were shrinking and she felt another panic attack coming on.

Just as she was about to bang on Jon's door and get help, her cell phone rang Ryan's ringtone. Scrambling to the bed where she had thrown her clutch, she dug in the small purse and found her phone. Answering it, she waited to hear him.

"Courtney," his voice was cautious and her stomach flipped then fell to her feet. "Are you okay, baby? Uncle Jon called me and told me what happened. Are you okay?"

She let out a little yelp and slid to the floor. "I love you," she said over and over again.

"Shh shh, I know that, baby," he crooned. "Uncle Jon said you might be a bit upset. Tell me why you're upset, Courtney."

"Because of what he did," she shouted. "He's demanding I flirt and use what wiles I have to get information from the chief. He didn't even ask, Ryan, he just ordered me."

"That doesn't sound like Uncle Jon," Ryan began. "I'm sure what he meant was to throw out ideas and see what would work. You guys are in a tough place right now. Do you feel like he's using you? Violating you in some way?" Ryan was calm.

"No, of course not, but yes he is using me," she replied.

"If he had asked would you have done it?" Ryan asked.

"Not without some answers," she replied. "I don't want anyone but you, Ryan. God, why doesn't anyone believe that?"

"I believe it, baby," he calmed. "But I need to understand why you're so upset."

"Because he should have asked me," she answered.

"Is that the only reason?" he pressed gently. Courtney sighed, she couldn't tell him. "You enjoyed it, didn't you? The kiss, you enjoyed it," Ryan offered softly.

She hit her forehead with the palm of her hand. Tears streamed down her cheeks. "I wanted it to be you but it wasn't."

"And you enjoyed it," Ryan pushed. "Knowing it was Uncle Jon, you enjoyed it."

"I don't know," she replied.

"You do know," Ryan answered gently.

"I'm scared," she admitted.

"I know," he stated. "But how do you think Uncle Jon feels?"

"I don't give a damn about how he feels," she answered.

"No, think about it," he said. "Here, he has Beth, a very beautiful woman about to be his wife, someone he has history with that you and I couldn't even fathom. Now this young gorgeous woman enters his life reminding him every moment of the one thing he can't have, his dead wife. Don't lie to yourself, Courtney, you are so much like Aunt Carol. Yet this woman chose his nephew, a man who is like a son to him, to love and eventually marry. He knows what he should be feeling, but he doesn't because every time he looks at you he's reminded of a pain no living soul should ever have to experience. When he hears this young woman cares for him too, well, there's not much he can do. Think about that. Don't beat yourself up over it. It happened. Move on. The sooner you do that, the sooner you can be back with me. And not to be arrogant, but that's what you really want, isn't it?"

"More than anything," she answered.

"Then get to that point," Ryan urged. "I want to hold you and make love to you and be there for you more than you know. Considering we have spent this last month constantly in each other's company, this is killing me, baby I need you too. Now will you do me a favor? Go to Uncle Jon and tell him you understand. He needs to know he hasn't lost you completely. He's walking on eggshells because he doesn't want to ignite a panic attack, he doesn't realize that by doing that it only makes you angry. You don't like anyone treating you differently. Me, that's different, but anyone else around you, you want them to treat you the same way as before.

"Uncle Jon doesn't know to do that. He let his guard down for a second and though I agree his method was sorely lacking, that's who he is. He thinks you're upset because of the kiss and he feels horrible, but what he doesn't understand is you're scared. Please, honey, he needs to know you're still you. Show him you're still his partner. If he doesn't know that you are strong and ready to tackle to world again then he needs to see it. He is so worried about you. He still talks about it to me and how it nearly killed him not to go after you. Go to him and tell him to stop walking on eggshells. Buck up and be the woman I know you can be."

"What if I'm not as strong as I was? What if Dave was right? I shouldn't have come back yet."

"You know all I heard in that? What if... what if you are?"

Courtney was quiet for a moment then sighed. "I love you," she said.

"I know," he said smugly. "Now are you okay?"

"Better," she answered. "I was on the verge of a breakdown before you called."

"I figured," he replied. "But you are one of the strongest women I know and he needs to see that side of you. He loves you too, baby. He just doesn't know you as well as I do."

"You are so smug," she teased.

"I'm just telling the truth," she heard the grin on his face. "Now go, the sooner you two get this straightened out, the sooner you're back in my arms."

"That is an incentive I can agree to," she answered. "I love you and I will be home soon."

"Just promise me you'll take care of yourself," he said. "I don't care who you have to flirt with or even kiss as long as every night it's me you dream about."

"Always has been and always will be, Ryan. I love you," she promised.

Chapter
Fourteen

Courtney knocked on her adjoining door not wanting to burst in. Hearing Jon's muffled voice telling her to enter, she slowly turned the knob and opened the door. Not seeing him at first, her eyes caught the light of the floor lamp by the chair beside the window.

Jon sat in the wingback chair, a book in his lap, his glasses halfway down his nose, and a glass of whiskey at his elbow, looking every bit the college professor. His gaze was a mixture of unease, expectation and apology.

"Hey," she started.

"Hello," he replied.

"Ryan called," she went on. "He said you called and told him what had happened."

"I did," Jon replied.

"Thank you," she said.

"You're welcome."

She shifted from one foot to the other and flashes of being in her professors' offices came back to her. But so did Ryan's words. Putting her shoulders back, she looked him in the eye.

"I'm sorry I got upset," she stated. "I am not upset about you yanking me into a darkened corner and kissing me, but I don't like you thinking I'll use my wiles on anyone. Those men creep me out. I wish you had asked me. The way you said it made me think you thought of me as merely a pawn, someone who will jump into bed with anyone. News flash but it's only ever been Ryan." She felt her cheeks flame as that slipped out.

"I understand," Jon answered not saying anything more about it. "I am sorry you were under that impression but that is not what I meant. My mind was going to the possibilities Pellegrino had us tailed and possibly our room searched. And I was right," he tossed a plastic baggie to her. She caught the bag and studied the object inside.

The little antennae told her immediately what it was. She looked up at Jon.

"Is it dead?" she asked.

"Yes, I made sure," he replied. "But someone planted it right here," he motioned to the inside of the lamp shade above his left shoulder. "They obviously liked you and my thoughts went to how can we get them to open up without a court order. But if it makes you uncomfortable then I understand. We will not use that. I don't think you're easy, I don't think you sleep around. I merely thought we could use what weapons we have. I'm sorry if you thought I meant it differently."

"God, what a partner I am," she huffed and sat down on the bed.

"What do you mean by that?"

"I'm twenty-seven, you would think I would understand what you meant and not thrown a tantrum like a six year old."

"You have been through hell," Jon reminded her.

"It's no excuse," she stated.

Jon breathed a laugh, "it's every excuse. Courtney, you nearly died and I didn't do a damn thing about it."

"There was nothing you could do, Jon," she reassured him.

"That's not true and we both know it," he said. "But you're safe and everything it okay now. What we need to do is find our footing again. I understand why you don't trust me anymore but it's killing me to know you would think the worst of me."

"What?" she breathed. "What are you talking about?"

"Last year, hell two months ago you would never have believed I thought you were easy. But now you think the worst of me and I have only myself to blame."

"Stop it," Courtney stood. "You don't get to take the blame. Dammit, Jon I do believe and trust in you. What happened a month ago, happened. It's over. Don't go borrowing trouble."

When Jon didn't look up at her, she knelt beside him. "You made a decision, yes. I made a decision. It caused a lot of worry and pain, but put the blame where it belongs. It's Rob, or Paul or whatever his name is. It's on him. I don't blame you. I don't blame me. It's over. My only concern is," she looked down and lowered her voice. "It'll be the first time I'll be sleeping in a bed without Ryan after what happened. I know that's weird, maybe even gross, and I know it hasn't been that long but I'm worried the…"

"You're afraid the nightmares will start up again without him. He grounds you and without him beside you, you worry you'll give into the fear that constantly surrounds you."

"Sounds like you've been there," she said.

Jon waited until she looked up at him. "I have."

Courtney fell silent and looked away. "I'm sorry," she whispered.

Jon didn't reply to her apology instead he closed the book, set it aside, grabbed her hands and helped her stand.

"Listen," he began looking down at her. "I don't want you to worry about the nightmares so long as I'm here. Leave your door propped open so if you need me I can be there in seconds. I know what it's like to have fear hanging over you. I have been there, Courtney." Reaching out, his eyes questioned if she would step back. He rubbed his hands over her arms when she stepped into him. "Now, it's late, we've had an… interesting day. The drive is catching up to me. Get some sleep and know I am here. If you need me, you just call my name and I'll be there faster than the wee folk can drink whiskey."

She laughed once. "I don't know what that means but I'm

guessing that's pretty fast."

"Pretty damn fast, yeah," he answered. "Now, get to bed."

"Are we okay?" she asked before she broke the connection between them.

"Definitely," he replied.

"I appreciate you calling Ryan," she said.

"Always," he kissed her forehead and watched as she walked to her room, closing the door slightly.

Chapter Fifteen

"Any word from Zoe?" Steven asked HQ when he checked in.

"Nothing yet," Mac answered. "But she's dark so it makes sense."

"Let me know when she calls in, okay?" Steven replied.

"Will do," he promised and then hung up. As Steven looked down the long aisle of an empty church, he heaved a sigh. Zoe missed her check-in a day ago and he was starting to worry. She hadn't missed a check-in in the nearly five years he'd known her. Last he had heard from her, O'Malley senior had taken the bait and she was officially his mistress. But that was it. Tapping the phone against his palm, he hated he wasn't in the field anymore but as Amber's and Josh's faces flashed across his mind, he knew he couldn't risk it. Especially now Amber was pregnant.

He was going to be a father.

That thought sobered him far more than any other. At thirty-seven he never thought he would be a father except to maybe an adopted son such as Josh. But there was no mistaking his girlfriend, nearly his fiancée, was pregnant and the engagement ring was burning a hole in his dresser. He had to finish this mission before he could pledge his life to her. It was to be his last. He was retiring. Turning his hand to writing, he already had a draft of a manuscript he thought about asking his mother to present to her agent. But the CIA would never allow him to publish a book while still on their payroll. And he was still on their payroll until all his agents were back safe and sound.

"Dammit Zoe, where are you?" he breathed then looked up at the cross hanging behind the pulpit and mumbled an apology.

<hr />

Courtney slowly woke the next morning and looked around her, taking a moment to remember where she was. The alarm clock read 8:30 and she grabbed her phone to check for any messages. She had two texts one from Jon and one from Ryan.

Ryan: Good morning, beautiful. Just remember I love you and I can't wait until we're back together. I have some interesting ideas to try out ;-)

Grinning, she typed out a reply that made her blush but she wanted him to be thinking about her all day. Ryan's response was the shocked emoji and she laughed. Getting up, she headed to the shower and checked the other text.

Jon: Went down to the gym for an hour, will be back up before breakfast is over. Meet me in the breakfast room? 8:45?

The text had been sent at six that morning. Knocking on the door and slowly pushing it open when there was no answer, Jon's room was empty. Sending a quick text back, she asked to push breakfast to nine as she had just gotten up. Before she stepped into the shower, her phone buzzed on the toilet seat.

Jon: Sounds good, let me know when you're on your way. I'll get a table, it's pretty busy, oh and the coffee sucks.

She chuckled, grateful they could return to their banter and texted back.

Courtney: So says the man who drinks six shots of espresso in the morning.

Jon: Four, and it's not my fault! I've been spoiled by strong coffee. Blame Mat for that one!

Mat, their former captain, Jon's brother-in-law and best friend, had been caught up in a scandal about three months ago and had fled to Spain, his home. Jon still worked to clear his name, but as budget cuts hit, he was working without the cooperation of the IMPD.

Courtney sent a smiley face back and stepped into the shower. The hot water felt good but stifling. Cutting her usual twenty minute shower down to ten, she got out and immediately turned on the exhaust fan. Staring at her blurred image in the fogged mirror, her hands trembled and her heart pounded.

"No, not again," she breathed. The humidity in the bathroom was overpowering and she couldn't breathe. "Calm down, calm down, calm down," she kept repeating over and over again. Opening the door, she stepped out of the bathroom and raced to her luggage pulling out something to wear. The air was on but she still couldn't catch her breath, it was as if something had grabbed hold of her and wouldn't let her go. Her entire body shook as she pulled on some sweats and a t-shirt. She couldn't calm down. She was about to lose it and there was nothing she could do. Grabbing her phone, she dialed as quickly as her trembling hands would allow.

"On your way?" Jon's voice came over the phone.

"Jon, help, please," was all she could say before the fear overpowered her.

Courtney woke with a pair of arms around her and wrapped in a blanket. She was resting on something soft and someone with a very soothing deep voice was stroking her hair and humming a song from Jane Eyre, the musical she and Jon starred in when they first met. Taking a deep breath, she recognized the cologne.

"Jon," she breathed.

The humming stopped and Jon leaned over her. "Hey," he answered. "How are you feeling?"

"What happened?" she asked realizing he held her in her bed.

"What do you remember?" he prompted.

"I was about to have a panic attack and I called you," she answered.

"That was three hours ago," he replied. "I got up here as fast as I could and found you balled up in the corner. You were awake but I don't think you were here, if you know what I mean." She nodded and slowly leaned up. Jon helped situate the pillows behind her so she could rest against the headboard. Once she was settled, he sat up beside her and continued. "When you finally realized I wasn't a threat, you let me close and I was able to get you here. You passed out."

Swallowing, her throat was raw and she vaguely remembered screaming. Her eyes slowly turned to Jon and saw a bruise darkening his cheek bone. She reached over and gently touched it.

"Did I do that?" she asked. He didn't answer right away but when she pulled his face back to hers, he nodded. "I'm sorry," she said.

"It wasn't you, I approached too quickly," he answered. "It's been a while since I dealt with PTSD and I forgot what to do."

"I know. I'm sorry. I'm working through it, but sometimes I can't control it," she admitted.

"Hey, it's okay," he said. "A lot of people go through that. More than you know. How are you feeling now?"

"A little sore," she admitted. "I guess breakfast is over if it's nearly noon, huh?"

"Yeah," he answered. "But we can order room service."

"What time were we supposed to meet with the chief?" she asked.

"I called him while you were resting and mentioned something came up and see if we could meet him at two," Jon said.

"Okay," she answered. "Then maybe room service is a good idea."

"Do you want to get out of here?" Jon asked. "I know sometimes fresh air helps."

"That sounds even better," she agreed. "It's stuffy."

"Stay here while I get you something to wear," he slipped off the bed and went to her suit case lying open on the floor. "Jeans and this shirt okay?" he pulled them out.

"Perfect," she said. Without saying anything, he pulled out a bra for her and handed her the clothes. She didn't want to know how he knew she wasn't wearing one. "Thanks," she mumbled as he walked over to her. Offering to help her up, he held her elbows until she was firmly on her feet. He took a step back and turned away from her. Quickly, she pulled on the clothes and called to him when she finished.

"Let's head out, I want you to have fresh air soon, your color isn't back yet," he said. "And I don't like that your hands are still shaking."

She clenched her fists to try and stop it, but it didn't help. Nodding, she found her tennis shoes and pulled them on.

Chapter Sixteen

Brent took off his glasses and pinched the bridge of his nose. He had been up for a solid eighteen hours and was counting down the seconds until Danny took over for him. Meredith had texted him saying his replacement would be there to relieve him in twenty-five minutes, that was twenty minutes ago. He massaged his forehead just above his right eyebrow with the palm of his right hand and put his glasses back on. Then, looking down at the makeup that discolored his palm, he cursed. Checking his face in the mirror, he noticed the distinguishing mark on his forehead just above his eyebrow, clear as day.

"Dammit," he muttered. Quickly reapplying the makeup, he had just finished when there was a knock at the door of his van.

"Who is it?" He called.

"Wild rover," came the answer.

Opening the door to Danny Rosslyn, codename *Wild Rover* after the song, he sat back and watched the Northern Irishman close the door behind him.

"Any news?" Danny asked his thick Belfastian accent showing through.

"None," Brent answered.

"Any update on Phoenix?" He asked after Zoe.

"Not that I know," he answered. "I know Casanova is starting to worry."

"After we saw Jon and Courtney in the pub, I was worried the gig was up. But O'Malley is probably keeping her to himself," he answered. "At least no news is good news, right?"

"Not usually," Brent answered rubbing his eyes again.

"You look tired," Danny said.

"Exhausted," he answered.

"Give me the run down and take a nap," Danny said looking at the screens.

"They went for burgers and are talking about PTSD," Brent replied.

"Give me the report you will give Meredith."

"I couldn't place the bug, although I did place Casanova's," he admitted. "Jon and Courtney are sleeping together, even though we know they're not. And they're about to head to the precinct to go over Donna Cross's file."

"Good, okay," Danny said. "Zachary is dead."

"Seriously? Damn," Brent asked.

"He killed him when he was caught by Jon sneaking out of the room," Danny replied.

"But I thought Jon pretended not to see him," Brent said.

"I thought so too, but Zachary wasn't so sure and Meredith ordered his death," he answered.

"Wow," he breathed. "Watch your back,"

"You are closer to them than I am," Danny said. "I'm working on the O'Malley gang. I can't let Eammon O'Malley see me."

"You know," Brent started. "You never did say how you know him."

"No, I didn't," he answered and turned back.

"Okay," Brent dragged out. He was too tired to play a game. "I'm going to my room."

Brent headed for the back door of the van, when he heard, "Shadow," Danny started. He turned back. "I know him from my days in the NSIS."

"I know there's more than just working a case about him, Dan," Brent said. "When you're ready. If you're ready, I'm here to listen."

They didn't say any more and Danny watched first in person then on the screen as Brent left the van, crossed the street and went into the hotel.

Closing his eyes at the pain building inside his chest, he clutched the necklace he wore and, as usual, it calmed him. Shaking his head and squeezing his eyes closed, he shut out the screams he heard as clear as day. They were old screams, screams that haunted him any time O'Malley was mentioned. As usual, he muttered a curse and opened his eyes looking at the mug shot of his nemesis.

"I'll get you, you bastard," he said. "I'll make you pay for what you stole from me, mark my words."

Once his ritual of calming down from his memories was over, he put on the headset and listened to the conversation using the speaker on Jon's phone.

"You know when a cop has a gut feeling something is off?" Courtney asked as they sat at an old sixties diner waiting on their hamburgers.

"Yeah," Jon answered and promptly hiccupped from the soda fountain coke he just sipped.

"I feel someone watching us," she said.

"Yeah, I have it too," he replied.

"And with that bug, someone wants to know what we talk about," she said.

"We've not made anything a secret. But," he reasoned. "Whatever we say to each other behind closed doors and what we say out in the open could be two completely different things. Someone wants in on our private conversations."

"But who could it be?" She asked. "The chief? The PR guy? Those are the only ones who knew we'd be out of the hotel rooms last night."

"Not necessarily true," Jon answered, leaning back as their burgers were placed before them. "For now, let's not say anything about the bug. I have a contact for unsanctioned goods. I'm sure he can get me a bug sweeper. And let's make it known we will use your room to talk not mine."

"Talk and other things since they think we're sleeping together," Courtney replied placing the napkin on her lap.

"Are you okay with that?" Jon asked.

"It's what needs to be done," she answered. "But I need to know one thing. Are you and, more importantly, Beth going to be all right with what I will do? If we're really to act like we are a couple, then we need to be a couple in all ways. Will she be all right with me kissing you, flirting with you, touching you in a way only a girlfriend should?"

"Beth is used to me being a cop. So long as we don't actually sleep together, she'll be fine."

"Good, then we are agreed," she said.

"Good," Jon answered. "Now can I enjoy my cheeseburger without thinking about sex?"

"I don't know, you're a man, might be difficult for you," she laughed.

Jon didn't dignify a response and merely took a big bite of the hamburger and moaned as the burst of flavor hit his taste buds.

"If you're finished with your love affair with the burger, did you want to contact your guy for the bug sweeper?" Courtney asked.

"I'm a little busy at the moment," he teased.

"Get a room," she laughed taking a bite of her burger. He pulled out his cell phone and dialed.

"Steven," he grinned when he answered the phone. Courtney laughed and shook her head. "Did I catch you at a good time?"

———————

Jon and Courtney were escorted through the precinct to the chief who stood and greeted them in his usual friendly way. Offering them a seat, he slid the file over.

"This is everything we have on Donna Cross," Pellegrino stated.

Jon took the file off the desk and opened it. Courtney placed her hand on his leg, a little too high for his comfort, but he knew what she was doing. He leaned toward her and winked at her.

"'COD was single GSW to the head," Jon read aloud. "Lacerations on her wrists and ankles suggesting she was bound. Slight bruising around her mouth indicating the presence of a gag for some amount of time. No signs of any other bruising or sexual assault. Coagulation of blood suggests death was only a few minutes before she was found. Fibers found on her hair and skin of her forearm were wool.' Any indication as to where she was held?" Jon looked up.

"Not yet," Pellegrino said, his eyes on Courtney's hand on Jon's leg. Snapping his eyes up, he continued. "I have my men sweeping their beats for anything suspicious and any place that could have been used as a holding cell. So far we've come up empty."

"Could we see the body?" He asked.

"If you want," Pellegrino replied.

"I trust your M.E. but I have something specific I'm looking for." Jon explained.

"Fair enough," Pellegrino replied standing. Jon and Courtney stood too and Jon extended his hand to the chief.

"I want to thank you, sir for being so willing to help us with Judge Cross's murder. He was a state treasure and his death is a national tragedy," Jon stated. Courtney recognized the Mayor's words.

"Of course," he answered. "We're all in this together. Now if there's anything else I can help with please, don't hesitate to ask me. I have asked the detectives in charge to meet you downstairs. They are open to speaking with you."

"Thank you," Jon said. "Could we get a copy of this file? My partner and I work better talking things out."

"We can use my room," Courtney said catching her cue.

"We could use mine too," he answered as she expected.

"Yeah, but mine is probably cleaner and… more fun," she winked. Jon paused.

"Fair enough," he replied.

"You have separate rooms?" the chief asked.

Jon looked over at him. "Of course," he answered, tapping the side of his nose.

"Ah… of course," he replied. "My lips are sealed."

"We appreciate it," Jon pulled Courtney into his side and she placed her hand on his chest. "And now that is cleared up, I would like to see Donna's body please."

"Of course," Pellegrino pressed a button on his desk phone. "Harris, come in here please."

"On my way, Sir," Kyle's voice said over the speaker. The door opened a moment later and the PR director walked in. Courtney pulled away from Jon to smile flirtatiously at the PR director. Kyle eyed her up and down and winked. Jon hated the outfit she wore, but her argument was valid. They had gone shopping after their lunch and she had picked out the tightest pants she could manage and a low scooping shirt with a pushup bra. She had styled her brown hair with blonde highlights and a blowout. The silky tresses fell passed her shoulders in luscious layers. She looked beautiful and dangerous, exactly what the two men seemed to like.

"It's good to see you again, detective," Kyle Harris said.

"Please, Kyle, what did I say?" She lowered her voice to a husky tone that made Jon's hand clench. "It's Courtney when I'm out of uniform,"

"I would very much like to see you out of uniform," Kyle winked.

Jon cleared his throat and Kyle's eyes snapped to his.

"Sorry, but your partner is hot," Kyle said.

"Kyle, please. Escort the lieutenant and detective to the morgue. I'll call Dr. Williams and let him know you're on your way,"

Adam Pellegrino said. "And Burns and Martin should meet you there."

"Thank you," Jon answered as he pulled Courtney into his side a little too tightly. She giggled and leaned in to whisper something in his ear.

"Pretend I just said something only a lover would say," she said to him. Jon did, giving the best performance he could. Laughing, he smirked and tapped her backside with the file as she walked out.

Chapter Seventeen

Meeting with the two detectives Burns and Martin in the morgue, they explained so far they had nothing to go on. Apparently, those they spoke with said Donna was well liked and lived in the suburbs of Minneapolis. When they had gone to her house, there was a car in the drive but no answer. However, they did say they saw the curtains move in the living room.

Asking for the address and permission to go themselves, Jon and Courtney walked out of the main doors of the precinct three hours later, to be greeted by a downpour of rain. As they waited under the overhang for a moment, Jon shrugged out of his coat and dropped it over her shoulders.

"Thanks," she shivered. "And I appreciate the outfit." She looked down.

"Yeah," he sighed. "About that," he pulled the coat tighter

around her shoulders as she laughed.

"It worked, didn't it?" she beamed. "And Kyle asked me out on a date."

"Seriously? When?" Jon demanded.

"Well we haven't worked out the details yet but..."

"When did he ask you? I was with you the entire time," Jon said.

"My my, if I didn't know any better I would think you're jealous," she sing-songed walking her fingers up his shoulder to flick his stubble covered chin.

"You know what I mean," Jon said.

"I do and I think it's cute," she laughed. "He asked me while you and the detectives were having your little side bar conversation about Donna's tattoo."

"Cheeky bastard," Jon mumbled.

"Are you saying I don't deserve his attentions?" she teased.

"I'm saying any man who only wants you for your body is a fool, you have a mind unlike anyone else and a wit, steadfastness, and loyalty that should be loved. I hate men who look at merely the body. The body withers. But a mind, a mind is a precious thing."

Courtney stared up at him and took his hand in hers. "I think I just fell back in love with you," she said.

"Courtney, that's not what I—"

"I know, but you are an amazing man, Jonathan Greene and I am truly blessed to have you as a partner. You have taught Ryan to be just like you and that's one of the things I love about him."

Reaching up she kissed his cheek. "Now, what would you like to do?"

Taking a deep breath, Jon filled his lungs with the smell of fresh rain. "You know it's days like today I miss Ireland and also going to the Art Museum," Jon said.

"The art museum?"

"Yeah you know the one by Butler?" Jon replied.

"Oh, I know what art museum you meant, but I just didn't expect it to be your special hang out."

"There is a good reason," he answered.

"Ah," she replied. "And here I thought you wanted to get in touch with your artsy side."

"Can't a grown man enjoy art?" He teased.

"Not without alcohol," she smiled.

"Oh, very true," he replied.

———————◦◦◦———————

Danny zoomed in and squinted trying to make out what Jon was holding in his hand as he pulled off his jacket and draped it over Courtney's shoulders. He couldn't make out what it was but it looked like a file. Picking up his pen, he made a note of the time and what he saw. Then, pulling out his phone, he texted a number. Leaving out what he had read on their lips, he told Meredith what he had seen. She responded almost immediately to tell him to keep on their tail. She wanted to know where they were going. Well, he wasn't about to tell her. The art museum was the safe haven for the agents on his team. But he did pull out his other phone and sent a text to Steven. Did he want him to follow them for protection in case things went south or did he want him to lay low? His phone buzzed on the counter and glancing at it, he nodded.

Cas: The art museum is covered, lay low.

He pushed back from the monitors and sighed seeing the downpour outside and hearing the large rain drops blink against the roof.

"God, I miss Ireland," he said. Grabbing his coffee mug, he took a drink and promptly spit it back into the cup wiping his mouth in disgust. It was ice cold. Just as he was about to pour it out and get another cup, his phone buzzed with another text.

Cas: Oh Danny boy the pipes the pipes are calling…

Rover: From glen to glen and down the mountain side…

Cas: Thirty minutes.

He pulled himself up to the front of the van and into the driver's seat. Once situated, he pulled into the traffic and drove to the meeting point.

Chapter Eighteen

Jon and Courtney walked through the lobby of the Minneapolis Art Museum and toward the main gallery. Jon paused a moment, looking at a sign just outside the doors.

"What's up?" Courtney asking walking back to him.

"Police Gala tonight," Jon explained indicating the sign. "Wonder if we could get an invite. Might prove promising."

"Sounds like fun, but the only dress I brought with me was the one I wore last night and that's not exactly *gala* worthy," she said as they pushed open the door to the main gallery.

"And I didn't bring my tux," he whispered as he saw a sign requesting the patrons to be quiet and respectful others.

"Why do you want to go?" She whispered back.

"Gut feeling," he answered. "And I wanted to give them a chance to bug your hotel room… if it is the chief, that is."

Courtney nodded. "Well, then use your charm and get us two tickets."

"At the moment, you have more sway over the PR Director, think you could swing it?" he asked.

"Probably, but then I would be indebted to him and I really don't want that," Courtney said. "He may want sex and when I refuse, it could end up being a problem."

"True. I'll call Dave," Jon replied. "Looks like we might need three tickets," he went on, something catching his eye and a smile breaking across his lips. Courtney followed his gaze to see Steven walking toward them.

"You got here quickly," she grinned. Steven and Amber had been frequent visitors when she and Ryan entertained. Courtney also figured out Amber was pregnant though she kept her suspicions to herself. Seeing Steven and Ryan together had helped her overcome some of the hardest memories of the pendulum.

"I thought I made myself clear, Jon," Steven hissed. "Stay out of this."

"I'm not in anything," Jon replied innocently.

"Don't give me that," Steven answered. Putting his hands on his hips, he huffed. "I really can't handle this stress. When I tell you to stay out of something I wish you would understand I am saying it for more reasons than you know."

"What's going on, Steven?" Jon asked.

Huffing, he looked from one to the other.

"Not here," he said and beckoned them to follow him.

Rounding a corner to a gallery of an old Italian master where caution tape was set up and the milky white plastic sheeting barricaded the entrance, he ducked under the tape and held it up for them to follow. The room was covered with electronics and two people, a man and woman looked up when Steven walked in. They eyed Jon and Courtney suspiciously but said nothing. Seeing several monitors and two of them set up to tape their hotel room floor and rooms, Jon looked over at his future stepson.

"What the hell is going on, Steven?"

"You've been watching us?" Courtney demanded. "I've showered and changed in that room you pervert!"

"We're not some Peeping Tom, Courtney," Steven said. "We don't have your room nor Jon's bathroom videotaped. But this is what you are encroaching on," he slapped down a three-ring binder three inches thick filled with files. "Everything is planned and you are the wild card. We don't know what you're up to. But yes, we have had your rooms monitored and I won't apologize for it."

"Then read us in, Steven," Courtney demanded. "You know we're good. Let us help you."

"I can't risk any more lives," Steven answered. "I wish I could."

"Then do it," Jon said. "We might be able to help you."

"I can't read you in on all of it, but I can tell you, if you want to help, get me dirt on Pellegrino."

"The police chief?"

"Yeah," Steven said. "He's neck deep in this but I don't know his role."

"You better start at the beginning," Jon crossed his arms over his chest.

"I'm now the handler for a group of agents and we're working on taking down the three heads of three separate mafias. Redorvsky is one, but there's also the Irish and the Italian. Dammit Jon, I can't have you meddling."

"I am not meddling," Jon stated. "If you had read us in to begin with none of this would have happened."

"Then go home now," Steven replied. "Quit while we're ahead. I have agents in the field who will die if you don't stop now."

Almost on que, something rang on one of the laptops. "Phoenix checking in."

"Shit," Steven cursed. Turning to them, he pursed his lips together. "We're not done but I have to take this."

Jon and Courtney took their leave and stepped back out passed the caution tape waiting for Steven to come out. Five minutes later, Steven's figure passed through the visqueen and he stood before them.

"We aren't ready to leave yet," Jon began. When Steven started to protest, he held up a hand and continued. "We're going to call Dave and get an invitation to the Police Gala tonight. We'll get you a ticket too."

"I've been trying for months to get into that party as an attendee," Steven replied. "I have two of my men as waiters but I couldn't get a ticket."

"See? Already helping," Courtney answered.

"Then why do you need a bug sweeper?" Steven asked.

"We have a feeling someone is going to bug our rooms," Courtney explained.

Steven's face fell into a cool mask of indifference and after a moment, Jon sighed. "Jaysus, where is it?" Steven looked up at him. "You and Beth have the same reactions when you don't want to give anything away."

"Look it was necessary," Steven defended.

"Where is it?" Jon asked again.

"Behind the lamp in Courtney's room. Between the lamp base and the wall."

"Well isn't that nice," Courtney said. "I wondered what that was."

"Thank you for not removing it," Steven replied. "And for not telling Jon."

"Yeah that's something we'll need to talk about, Courtney," Jon said. "But the bug sweeper is for another bug. I already found one in my room. You didn't bug mine, did you?"

"No," Steven replied. "I was going to have him do it later today."

"Don't," Jon said. "We have a theory we're testing."

"Then, here," Steven handed Jon a small rectangular device that almost looked like a remote to a TV.

"Thank you," Jon said pocketing it.

"Call me later?" Steven asked. "Let me know if you can get us into the gala tonight."

"Will do," Jon answered.

"Sorry, I have to leave you now, I have another meeting to get to," Steven popped the collar on his CPO jacket and walked through the art museum texting on his phone.

Chapter Nineteen

Acting Captain Dave Weston answered his desk phone on the fourth ring.

"Hello?" He asked absently without looking at the name.

"Well, good afternoon to you too," he heard and his ears perked up.

"What are you doing calling me?" he hissed.

"Am I not supposed to call?"

"No, not right now," Dave replied. "And especially not *this* number. You know it's not secure."

"It's secure enough for this conversation, Dad," the man said.

"Don't call me that, you know what's at stake here," Dave muttered.

"Okay, okay easy," he answered. "Look you're about to get

a call from Jon asking you to get them tickets to the Minneapolis Police Gala tonight. I need you to get two more without them knowing."

"And why? I told you when you signed up for this, I wasn't going to be your meal ticket," Dave said.

"I'm not asking for me, I'm asking for someone else," he replied.

"Then why didn't *he* call me?" Dave asked.

"Because he's busy," the man answered. "Come on, Dad, you know I never ask. Work with me here."

"It's not that I don't want to," Dave replied. "I have to keep a low profile here."

"I know, but do this as acting captain," the man said. "Trust me, it's important or I wouldn't risk breaking my cover to ask."

Dave sighed and rubbed a hand down his face. Leaning back in the chair, he nodded.

"Yeah, fine okay," Dave said. "What name should I ask for the other two to be in?"

"Sergeant Russell Davis," he replied.

"Seriously? Your *stepfather's* name?" Dave demanded.

"It's a name I recognize," he replied. "Do you want me to put it in my real name? Or yours?"

"Fine, I'll do what I can. Should I text or call you?"

"Neither," he answered. "Jon is going to call Steven when he gets off the phone with you. We'll know then."

"Good, the less chatter about this the better," Dave replied.

"I know," he said. "Thanks, Dad."

"Be careful," he asked. "You know what I can't say."

"Same here," he replied. "And I will be. I'll check in when it's over. Maybe we can take a trip together. I hear Paris is nice this time of year."

"Paris it is, then," he answered. "Just don't get shot."

"And miss out on all the fun? No thanks," he said. "Gotta go." The phone went dead and Dave bit his tongue to stop himself from calling his son's name over an open line. He wasn't there when his son was growing up but he was never supposed to be a father. He and his ex-wife were married only a year when Dave was accepted into Homeland Security and he knew a family was the last thing an ambitious agent could have. But that never stopped him from watching over his son as he grew up, even if it was in the shadows. Dave laughed humorlessly. Maybe that's why his son had chosen that name as his codename. *The Shadow.*

He jumped when the phone rang again. This time he checked the caller ID and saw Jon's name displayed.

"Jon," he leaned back in his chair when he answered and feigned a smiling tone. "How's the twin cities?"

"The same," Jon answered.

"That was just bad, man," Dave replied.

"Yeah, I know," Jon said laughing. "Dad joke."

"Find anything interesting?" Dave asked.

"They have a restaurant here that serves excellent Sushi, the hotel pool is pretty great and the art museum houses some excellent paintings," Jon replied.

"Glad to know you're enjoying yourself on your *working* vacation," Dave said.

"I'm calling because I could use your help," Jon replied.

"Naturally, I mean you clearly didn't call me to see how *my* day was going," Dave said. "So, what can I do for you?"

"Could you get us two tickets to the Police Gala tonight?" Jon asked.

"Well, I think so, but why?" Dave replied forcing his voice to sound surprised.

"Long story," Jon answered. "But I found a state issued bug in my room after seeing a man with a gun and badge leave my hotel room. I would like to find him and a benefit gala where all the cops or at least their photos will be around, just might be the best way of finding him."

"Well, I'll see what I can do. Be safe and send me your report tonight," Dave said.

"Yes, sir," Jon answered.

"Oh and Jon?" Dave called. "Try not to get too drunk tonight."

"Ha! No promises, but we'll attempt to behave ourselves… within reason," he replied.

Danny pulled into Mountainside Drive and saw the church in front of him. The modern structure clashed with the stained-glass window. In Ireland, he was used to five hundred to one thousand year old churches and if they weren't still functioning they were de-sanctified and turned into pubs. The church before him had a plaque stating it was one of the oldest churches in Minneapolis and it looked less than one hundred years old. He paused a moment to remember the church in his town of Antrim just west of Belfast. The stone structure had been on that spot for generations of his family and all of them had been christened there, even his own daughter. Clearing his throat, he pushed aside thoughts of her bouncy red hair and freckled face, a face he would never see again. Gritting his teeth against the pain, he got out of the van and headed into the church.

Dipping his finger in the Holy Water at the front and signing the cross on himself, Danny walked up the main aisle, slipping into one of the pews. He knelt and took out his rosary, holding it between his fingers, praying for those he had lost. Though he was born in Northern Ireland, he held to the faith of his parents, late wife and her family.

As he prayed, he kept his eyes open and watched any form of movement around him. Two old women a few pews in front of him and a man behind him, prayed. A family taking pictures, clearly tourists, walked aimlessly around the church. Then he saw his contact, dressed as a priest, walk across the lectern and head into the confessional. They locked eyes for a moment and Danny looked down before it became obvious.

After a suitable time had passed, Danny stood and headed

into the confessional.

"Bless me, Father for I have sinned it has been one month since my last confession," Danny said.

"What sins do you have to confess, son?" the priest asked.

"I've been a wild rover for manys a year and I spent all my money on whiskey and beer," Danny quoted from the song *Wild Rover*. The priest nodded and passed him a note through the holes in the wall between them.

"Three hail Mary's and one Our Father's," he said. Danny opened the note.

Tickets in the name of Sergeant Russell Davis. Black tie. Keep an eye out for O'Malley. Found out he's in town. Phoenix checked in. Skylark is going as planned.

Danny locked eyes with Steven through the confessional and nodded. Zoe had checked in. *Thank god.*

———⊷———

Steven adjusted his priest's collar as Danny left the confessional.

Why did this stupid thing have to itch so much? Steven wondered. His phone buzzed with a text from their techie back at HQ. Memorizing it, he deleted it quickly.

Mac: Movement in Russia's account. 500m to off shore account in Italian's name. Russian and Italian in communication.

Chapter Twenty

"Ready?" Jon knocked on the adjoining door after adjusting his bow tie.

"Ready," Courtney called. They had gone to the nearest dress and tuxedo shop earlier that day. Jon was fitted with a rental since he owned two tailormade for his six foot two inch frame back in Indiana. Courtney tried on dress after dress but none were right. They needed something elegant and yet showing her off for the Chief and PR Director to salivate the moment they saw her. When they finally found the perfect black silk dress, Jon purchased the items for them and they hurried back to the hotel to change.

Jon opened the adjoining door as Courtney grabbed her clutch off the bed and faced him.

"Wow," he stated. "You look beautiful." Her black silk gown hugged her body and fell straight to the floor. The front dipped but not too low and the sweeping back revealed almost all the way down to the curve of her backside.

"You look pretty fantastic yourself. You can really pull off the classic tuxedo, 007," she grinned.

"Greene, Jon Greene," he teased.

"It fits," she agreed.

"At fifty-six? I'll take it," then he reached back into his room, pulled out a long stemmed red rose and handed it to her.

"Hopeless romantic," she accepted it.

"Always," he replied. "You do look beautiful."

"Thank you," she answered. "I put my engagement ring in the safe but I'm a little leery of leaving it there."

"Wanna put it with mine?" he offered. "I have a few things in there already."

"You always travel with your passport, huh?"

"Of course, and my family crest ring," he rubbed his right ring finger where Courtney saw the dark gold signet ring he always wore on special occasions. "You can always use the safe in my room. The code is my birthday; day and year."

"I don't think I can count back that far," she said.

"Oh, shut up," Jon teased.

Courtney gave him the ring from her own safe and watched as he put it away. "So," she started leaning against the doorframe. "What's the game plan for tonight?"

"Try to find the dirt on Pellegrino like Steven asked."

"Will he be there?" Jon had called him while she was trying

on dresses but she didn't hear if he got the tickets.

"Yes, he said he'll be a little late but he'll be there. One of his other agents will sneak in as a waiter," Jon explained shutting the door of the safe.

"Do you think Pellegrino could be the other one their looking at getting? He did say three mafia heads. If Redorvsky is one, could Pellegrino be the other?"

"Italian?" Jon offered. "Possibly. Maybe that's what Steven needs our help figuring out."

"He's a cop," Courtney reasoned.

"A perfect cover?" Jon replied.

"I hate dirty cops. They give the rest of us bad names," she said.

"Agreed but let's wait to pass judgement until we know for certain," Jon stated and pulled on his coat.

Courtney adjusted the wrap they had picked up to go with the dress and Jon offered his arm.

"Whatever happens, promise me you'll be careful," Jon said.

"I promise," she replied. "We should have a code in case I can't get out of a situation and need your help."

"Okay, what were you thinking?" he asked.

"Not sure, maybe something like *could you get me a glass of wine?* or something like that."

"That could work," he replied. "But you like wine and might actually want one. How about bourbon? Don't you hate it?"

"Yuck, yes," she replied.

"Can't say I blame you," he chuckled. "But that's American and more power to those who like it. I could never get a taste for it meself," he said, his Irish accent showing through.

Courtney giggled as they waited for the elevator. "So we're agreed, if I need your help getting out of something, I ask you for a bourbon."

"Yes," Jon nodded. "Let's just hope it doesn't come to that."

"Let's hope."

"Ready, Casanova?" Danny called down the hall as he straightened his bow tie.

"Yeah," Steven answered and walked out of his room with his phone in his hand and a stupid grin on his face.

"Everything all right at home?" Danny asked.

Steven looked up and nodded. "Yep, nothing to worry about."

"Then why the stupid grin?" Danny asked.

"What stupid grin?" Steven answered. Danny looked at him pointedly and Steven sighed. "My fiancée just sent me another ultrasound picture of our kid," he said. "I was looking at it."

"Wanna share?" Danny asked.

"We're not women, Dan, we don't normally share pictures," Steven replied.

"Not of shoes and clothes, but kids? Yeah, you do," Danny answered. "And it'll be something nice to think about in this crazy arse world."

Steven stared at him for a little while then nodded and pulled out his phone. The black and white, grainy picture on the screen made Danny smile softly. It wasn't that long ago he had seen a similar picture and his heart swelled with pride just as Steven's probably was.

"Beautiful," he answered. "Do you know if it's a boy or a girl yet?"

"Not yet," he replied.

"Preference?"

"Healthy, preferably," Steven answered.

"Due date?"

"Valentine's Day actually," he said.

"Congrats," Danny looked away when memories bombarded him.

"You all right?" Steven asked.

"Aye," Danny replied quickly and cleared his throat. "Let's get going, we should be there before the party gets too crazy."

Chapter
Twenty-One

When Jon and Courtney arrived at the museum, Jon had the limousine driver keep the champagne he asked for on ice for their drive back. Jon gave the young woman at the gate their names and walked in with Courtney on his arm. Glancing over to the corner of the building, he noticed Steven standing just beyond in a tux with another man at his side. Not wanting to draw attention to them, he said nothing and walked in.

The main area was decked in police blue and silver. Couples mingled in the main lobby listening to the soft jazz music from the live band and drinking champagne and cocktails offered by the waiters dressed in black and white livery. Small tables dotted the room allowing couples to set their drinks and hors d'oeuvres down as they chatted.

Tuxedos and ball gowns lent a formal flare to the room. Jon

stopped at one of the empty tables on the outskirts of the room. A waiter came around and offered Champagne which they both accepted. Toasting each other, Courtney spotted the chief and Kyle Harris watching them. Jon's back was to them so she slid her hand over his chest and around his shoulder. He immediately understood and leaned into her. Placing a gentle kiss on his lips, she stroked the back of his hair with her hand and whispered, "They're watching us."

"I think everyone is watching us with you in that gown," he replied.

"You did say wow factor," she answered.

"And I think it was accomplished."

Giggling as if he said something else, she kissed him lightly again and stepped back when the chief walked up.

"Lieutenant! Detective! So glad you could make it!" Adam Pellegrino said walking up to them and shaking their hands. "I'm so sorry I didn't invite you myself. It completely slipped my mind. Please on behalf of the MPD accept our gratitude to your captain for his most generous donation. I'm glad you two were able to come. Detective, you look stunning."

"Thank you," she answered raising the champagne to her lips and slowly taking a drink not taking her eyes off of the chief. "And you look very handsome, Chief."

"Oh please," Adam waved her off. "I told you I'm rather unconventional. Adam, please."

"Adam," she answered. "Then you know I'm not in

uniform. It's Courtney."

"Courtney, it is," he said. "I've made it my mission tonight to dance with every beautiful woman in the room. Will you do me the honor?"

"I would be delighted," she answered.

Adam's eyes went to Jon. "As long as you don't mind," Adam said.

"Not at all, Chief," Jon replied. "We are indebted to you."

"It's not my place to report you, I too understand forbidden desire," he answered.

"Don't drink my champagne," Courtney tossed back at Jon.

"Or what?" Jon teased.

"I don't think you'll want to know," she said. "It definitely involves my handcuffs."

"Then in that case, I may enjoy it," Jon teased raising the glass to his lips and taking a small sip.

Laughing, Courtney left with Adam and as they entered the dancefloor, the chief pulled her close.

"How long as it been going on?" he asked.

"What?" she coyly removed an invisible speck of lint from the chief's jacket.

"You and your partner, I assume you're sleeping together," he said.

"I don't know what you mean," she locked eyes with him.

"You don't have to pretend with me," he said, his hand slipping down her open back to the curve of her ass.

"It's hard for a woman in a man's world, if the rest of the force found out, they would accuse me of sleeping around to secure my promotion," she said.

He gripped her tightly and pulled her closer.

"And did you?" he asked.

"Our chief isn't nearly as young and handsome as you, Adam," she answered. "But I am curious," she lowered her voice. "What would you do if someone on your force did want to sleep with you?"

"Who says I haven't?" he asked.

"A man like you? You could get any woman with a snap of his fingers."

Adam snapped his fingers. "Do I get you?" he asked.

Courtney laughed melodiously and shook her head.

"We may not be able to voice it, but we are together," her eyes drifting to Jon who had turned away from them.

"He would never know," he said.

"I would rather get to know you before I just jump into bed with you," she replied.

"And yet, you're only here for another two days," he said.

"True, but wouldn't you rather show me the sights of the city you protect?" she asked.

"Protect?" his voice was husky. "Who says I protect it?"

"Pretty much the badge you carry," she replied.

"The badge is a symbol," he answered. "Nothing more."

"As much as I love the good guy," she said. "I have to say

I've always had a soft spot for the bad guy."

"Then have a soft spot for me, because I am a *very* bad guy," he whispered before he lowered his lips to her neck and kissed.

The song ended before she could get more out of him. He twirled her around and walked with her back to Jon who stood chatting with another man Courtney didn't recognize but they weren't speaking English.

"Courtney," he smiled. "How was the dance? Did you want a bourbon?" His eyes searched hers to make sure she was all right. Courtney smiled and glanced over at Adam.

"Oh, not yet," she answered. "The chief is an excellent dancer. But it looks like you made a new friend."

"Yeah, I have," Jon replied giving her champagne back. Courtney couldn't help but hear Jon's Irish accent was a little more pronounced. Looking at the man beside him, his five foot ten inch frame was pleasing and reminded her of Ryan's physique. His light brown hair was cut short and his grey eyes seemed older than the rest of him. "Russell, let me introduce to you my partner Courtney Shields."

"It's nice to meet you," his Irish accent perked her ears. "You dance very well."

"Thank you, but I had a good leader," she winked at Adam.

"Well, I'm not one to boast," Adam said. "Forgive me, I don't think we've met."

"I'm sorry, Chief," Russell replied. "Sergeant Russell Davis from the sheriff's department. My friend Liam O'Malley sent me in his stead. He asked me to tell you something."

Adam nodded slowly and released Courtney.

"Forgive me, police business," he said motioning Russell to follow him.

Once alone, Jon turned to Courtney. "Are you all right?" he asked. "With all the touching, I wanted to punch him myself."

"Me too but I got some interesting information."

"Come dance with me," Jon said setting their glasses down and pulling her out on the dancefloor.

As the music drowned out their voices, Courtney told Jon about their exchange on the dancefloor.

"He's definitely involved deeper than he wants anyone to know," Courtney concluded.

"Doesn't surprise me," Jon said. "And Russell?" he nodded towards the two men in quiet conversation across the room. "Told me he works with Steven and asked for my help."

"Yeah, I thought you were speaking Irish," she replied.

Jon nodded. "Steven's here somewhere but if Russell needs help we're to create a distraction."

"What kind of distraction? I'm not exactly packing C-4 under this dress," she replied.

"We'll figure something out if the time comes," he answered as the song came to an end. "Can I get you something stronger than the champagne?"

"I'm good," she replied. "Go talk to the chief and see what you can get out of him. I'm going to go look around and see if I can find Kyle Harris, he might have more information."

"Be careful," Jon replied.

"I'll be fine," she answered and watched him walk toward the chief.

"Can I get you a refill, miss?" A waiter came by and offered.

"Thank you, yes," she answered. Her eyes lifted to the man handing her a drink and narrowed as she recognized him. "You?" she breathed.

"Shh," he said.

"You were at the gas station," she uttered.

"Yes," he answered.

"And the pub."

"Yes."

"Who are you?"

"I work with someone you know," he stated.

"Who?"

He looked at her pointedly then turned his gaze to where Steven walked into the room. Courtney gave nothing away with her eyes. She didn't know who he was and she wasn't about to let anyone know she knew Steven.

"You're good," he said. "But he asked me to tell you something. Meet him at the Police photo board near the band in twenty minutes."

"How do I know you're telling me the truth?" she demanded.

"Because he told me to tell you *once upon a midnight dreary while I pondered weak and weary."*

Courtney swallowed. "If he told you to say that, then he knew what it would do to me."

"He said you can handle it," he replied. "But he said you would know it was him and nothing else would convince you."

Courtney paused for a long moment and nodded.

"If you see him, tell him I will meet him there," she said.

"I will," he replied nodding and leaving as if they never spoke.

After calming her raging heartbeat, her blood pounding in her ears she was certain she would have another panic attack but for some reason she was able to calm herself down unlike before and when she locked eyes with Jon talking with Adam, she nodded once and walked into another room with a sign saying Old Dutch Masters. Aimlessly eyeing the paintings, she stopped at one painting in particular. The oil on canvas fascinated her.

The old woman in a chair, the browns, greys and blacks lent to the somberness of the painting but the look in the woman's eyes was one of fear as if she were on the verge of a panic attack herself. Somehow, staring at the painting calmed Courtney and she stood mesmerized for several minutes until someone walked up behind her and her back stiffened.

"Van Goyen, Woman in the chair, 1548, quite an interesting painting, don't you think?" Kyle Harris's voice stopped her from turning and taking the person down in a chokehold. Proud of herself for not jumping when he spoke, she continued to look at the painting as she replied

"1650 actually," she replied. "And it's not Van Goyen, it's Van Greyen, a common mistake with the two artists, but about there's about one hundred years difference between the two artists," she said.

"Beauty and brains," Harris said trailing a finger down her back. "Can't say I'm surprised."

"My mother was an art history major in college and has taught me everything I know. I practically grew up in an art museum," she explained.

"Downplaying your talent is not something you should do, Detective, especially when you're wearing a dress made for coming off."

"Oh, the dress will be coming off," she answered.

"And the lucky bastard who gets to see it?" he asked.

"That part is still to be decided," she replied. "But your chief is a healthy contender."

"Adam?" Kyle scoffed.

"Why not?" she asked. "He's a very handsome man."

"Yeah, I guess if you're into that," he replied.

"And why wouldn't I be into that?" she asked.

"Because you don't strike me as a woman blinded by power and status," he answered. "But rather, in want of a man who can keep up with you."

She turned to look at him.

"And that man is you?" She asked.

"Hey, don't let the blonde hair fool you, us Germans can keep up, sometimes better than the Italians," he replied.

"Maybe I like a little danger," she said.

"Honey, you don't know danger until I've been in your bed," he answered.

Slowly wrapping her arms around his neck, she locked eyes with him.

"Maybe I like it outside of the bedroom too," she whispered her voice husky. "And when it comes to a Police Chief versus a PR person, the chief will win out every time."

"Sometimes, you flirt with danger and you'll get burned," he said.

"I doubt the chief is that dangerous," she replied.

"You'd be surprised," he answered.

"Surprise me then," she replied. Before she realized what he was going to do, he pulled her close and pressed his lips onto hers. Once he broke away, she pulled back and slapped him. Stumbling back, he held his cheek.

"Dammit woman, what the hell was that for?"

"Surprise," she said before walking away from him.

Racing after her, he pulled on her arm and pinned her against him.

"So, it's like that, huh?" he asked. "You like the stronger dominant type. Be careful what you wish for, Pellegrino is dangerous and not just because he's chief. There's a side to him this city has never seen but they have seen the results from it."

"Oh? What is he, some kind of mob boss?" her eyes flashed with what she hoped was desire.

"Not for me to let the proverbial cat out of the bag, but listen honey, if you want him, be prepared to dance with the devil."

"Now now, no need to be jealous," she answered. Then looking down at her cleavage, she prevented her grin as his eyes followed hers. "Can I let you in on a secret?" He nodded and swallowed thickly. "I find you the more attractive of the two and if I didn't have to deal with my partner I'd not think twice about taking you back to the hotel."

His eyes snapped up to hers. "Does he need to know? You're an adult."

She made her laugh be a tinkle and smiled when a shiver ran down his back.

"I think he would have an issue with it," she answered. "We are a little more than partners."

"Then maybe I can sneak in," he offered.

"Has anyone ever told you that you try too hard?" she asked backing out of his embrace. Glancing over her shoulder as she walked away, Kyle had not moved. Finally, she reentered the main lobby area and Jon promptly took her now empty champagne glass and set it on the table, twirling her, he brought her back into his arms and slowly they swayed together.

"What happened?" he asked. "You were gone for a while."

"Found Kyle Harris," she admitted laying her head on his chest.

"And?" he asked.

"He propositioned me but he did tell me something interesting," she said.

"What's that?"

"He told me the Chief is dangerous and there's a side of him no one in this city has seen."

Jon said nothing as they danced a little longer but felt her slide against him.

"You all right?"

"I'm tired," she answered. "I'm tired of using my body to get information."

"You should've tried my job," Steven's voice came from behind her. She stopped moving with Jon and turned. "Did Brent give you my message?"

"Yeah, but I didn't appreciate it. I'm still not quite over everything, Steven, I could have had a panic attack," she scolded.

"I knew you were stronger than that," he replied. "Care to walk around a little? There's something I'd like to show you."

"Both of us or just me?" Courtney asked.

"Both," Steven replied. "There's a face I want you to see."

Jon and Courtney agreed and made their way following Steven around the outside of the dance floor and around near the band.

"I was supposed to meet you here," she said.

"Ten minutes ago," he replied. "But when I saw you leave the old masters' room, I figured you had a valid reason for not showing up."

"Sorry to disappoint," she answered.

"I will need to know what Harris said to you," he replied.

"You're not my handler, Steven," she spat. "And I've had about all I can handle of domineering men tonight."

Steven said nothing more until they were at the board with all the pictures of the police officers who could not attend the gala that evening.

"See anyone you recognize?" Steven asked.

"There," Jon said quietly. "The man named Sergeant Zachary Howard. He's the one I saw coming out of my room."

"He's dead," Steven replied. "My agent in the field overheard O'Malley talking about it over the phone and heard the name Howard. I needed to know if that was the face."

"He is, without a doubt, Steve," Jon answered.

Steven nodded and looked from one to the other.

"I need a distraction," he said. "I need to make my exit and I need you two to head back to the hotel."

"Where's your two men?" Jon asked.

"Danny is still here but he needs to tail Pellegrino and Brent is taking pictures. We have a report one of our marks is here."

"Who is it?" Courtney asked.

"I can't tell you that, Courtney you know that," he said.

"Dammit, Steven if you would just tell us what we need maybe we can help," Jon replied.

"You've done what you can," he answered. "And you have

given me information that could have taken a lot longer to get. Right now, I need to finish what I started. There are other things going on I can't tell you about. But don't be surprised if you see my two men following you. They are working for someone who wants you tailed."

"And who is that?" Jon asked.

"That's classified," he answered.

"Bullshit," Jon replied.

"Jon, I'm warning you, you need to stay out of this," Steven said. "There are things happening that can't be stopped. I'm trying to save you but I can't fight you too."

The two men stared each other down until Courtney placed a hand on Jon's arm.

"I'm getting pretty tired of the Alpha male bullshit, okay?" she said. "I've dealt with it a lot tonight. Let's go back to the hotel, have that champagne and order room service. We can regroup. We want to leave in two days anyway. So come on, what do you say, partner?"

Jon finally broke his stare down with Steven and looked at her.

"Fine," he answered. "Let's get going. We need to say our goodbyes to the chief."

"It's going to look odd, you leaving right after getting information about him," Steven offered.

"We have done this before, Steven we're not rookies," Jon said.

"I'm saying, it looks odd if you leave right after getting information about him *and* standing here talking to me."

"That's not my problem," Jon replied.

"Jon," Courtney said. "Don't."

"Fine, what do you suggest?" Jon demanded.

"Slap me," Steven said to Courtney.

"What?" Courtney looked at him.

"Slap me as if I propositioned you," he said.

"Both men propositioned me tonight," she replied. "They'll not find that convincing."

"Then make up a story at how I copped a feel," Steven answered.

"Without witnesses?" She asked.

"Fine," Steven huffed and reached forward, grabbing one of her breasts through the silk material. Courtney gasped and slapped him. Hard.

He stumbled back as most people in the room gasped and looked at them.

"How dare you!" She yelled. Jon pulled back and decked him. Steven went down like a sack of potatoes not as much of an act as he had hoped. Jon didn't pull his punch. Steven's jaw ached and he tasted blood.

"Get out!" Jon bellowed. "You're lucky I don't tear you to shreds."

The Chief and two others stepped forward placing a hand on Jon's shoulder which he promptly shrugged off.

"What happened here?" the power in Adam Pellegrino's voice surprised Courtney as she looked over at him.

"He's drunk and he... grabbed me," she said crossing her arms over her chest.

"Gregson, get him out of here and into a cab," Adam said. Jon put his arm around Courtney's shoulders. "Detective, are you all right?"

Courtney nodded. "He was a little too friendly." She looked up at Jon. "I could use a bourbon." Jon nodded slowly and pulled her tighter to him.

"Do you know him?" Adam asked as the cop bundled a stumbling drunk Steven out of the main room.

"Never seen him before," Courtney answered. "He came up to my partner and I as we were looking around, started a conversation and then just grabbed me."

"I am very sorry this happened on my watch, Detective," Adam said. "Would you like one of my men to escort you back to your hotel?"

"I'll do it," Kyle Harris stepped forward.

"That won't be necessary, Chief," Jon replied. "But if someone could call for the limo we arrived in? My partner and I will head out. Thank you for your generosity."

"Thank you both for coming. I'll see you in my office some time tomorrow?" He asked.

"We'll call when we're on our way," Jon offered.

"Excellent," he said. "I hope you enjoyed the evening,

Courtney."

"Until that moment," she replied. "I did... Adam."

The chief smirked and a slow wink closed one eye. Jon held her tighter to him and when the other cop who stepped up with the chief came back into the room to tell them that their limo had arrived, Jon turned Courtney to the door and together they walked out.

Chapter
Twenty-Two

"Are you hungry at all?" Jon asked as he closed the limo door behind him. "I mean I know they had hors d'oeuvres, but there wasn't anything substantial."

"I was thinking that cheeseburger place sounds awfully good, but we just had it. How about we go back to the hotel and order room service? I need to get out of this dress," she said.

"And me out of this penguin suit," Jon replied pulling one side of his bow tie and letting it hang around his neck. Next, the two buttons of his shirt were unbuttoned and he pulled off the coat. "Are you sure you're all right?"

"I can't believe he actually..." she trembled and crossed her arms tighter over her chest.

"I know," Jon stated. "He and I will have a stern conversation."

"He needed to, I understand, but warn me," she said.

"He took advantage of you and it was unacceptable," Jon answered.

"Just take me back to the hotel, Jon," she replied. "Could you hold me? I need someone's familiar touch to block out the feeling. I think I need to shower, I feel dirty."

Jon wrapped his arm around her shoulders and pulled her into him, kissing the top of her hair. "It's all right, I'm here."

———

Back at their hotel, Jon used the sweeper to see if the room was bugged and when they found nothing but the one Steven's team had placed, he put it away and gave Courtney back her engagement ring which she gratefully slipped on. Picking what they wanted from room service, Jon ordered while Courtney changed. The champagne Jon had ordered for the limo was chilling on ice with two glass flutes beside it. Once Courtney was changed she called Ryan while Jon pulled out of his tuxedo.

"Courtney?" Ryan's groggy voice answered the phone. "Is everything okay, baby?"

"Oh my god, Ryan I'm so sorry, I didn't think it was so late," she apologized.

"No, it's okay. It's not that late, I'm early rotation tomorrow, what's up?"

"We just got back from the gala and I wanted to call you," she said. "I didn't realize how late it was."

"I'm glad you did," he replied.

"How was work today?" she asked.

"Well, after I got your text all I could think about was you," he answered and she bit her lower lip. "You did that on purpose, didn't you?"

"Maybe," she teased. "It worked?"

"A little too well," he chuckled. "You are still coming home in a couple days, right?"

"That's the plan," she answered. "Jon and I are going to work from here a bit longer there's someone we need to see. But after that, yes."

"Promise when you get home, I'll have you all to myself for at least two nights," he teased.

"I can safely promise that, Dr. Marcellino," she said.

There was a knock at the door and someone called *room service*. Jon came back into her room changed into sweats and a black t-shirt and went to the door.

"I need to go, dinner's here," she said. "I love you."

"I love you too. Call me later?" he asked.

"Definitely," she answered and hung up as the hotel attendant rolled the cart into the room. After tipping him, Jon closed the door and joined Courtney at the dining table. "Wanna pop the bubbly?"

"Absolutely," he answered grabbing the bottle and prying the cork off with a loud pop. He poured as Courtney set out the utensils and covered plates. "Smells pretty good."

"It does," she agreed. "Room service is expensive but most of the time it's pretty darn good."

"Agreed," he answered. "When Scott, Ryan and I go to the Bahamas we always get room service the first night."

"I've seen pictures, it looks beautiful," she said sitting. "I think that's one place Ryan is thinking about taking me for our honeymoon."

"You would love it," he answered sitting next to her. "We always get the same suite when we go. It has three separate rooms, a common area and a kitchen. The balcony lines the entire suite and each of us have doors leading out to it. The view is gorgeous."

"I would love to go," she admitted. "But I also want to go back to Ireland or Scotland. It was so beautiful last time."

"You'll always go back to Ireland with us and Scotland isn't that far from there. We can always go there some other time. But in my opinion, a honeymoon is the beach and there's nothing quite like the Bahamas."

"Where did you go on your honeymoon?"

"Nassau Island," Jon replied. "Then over to Ireland, followed by a couple weeks in the Mediterranean on a yacht sailing around Spain and Italy."

"Okay, that's like the most perfect honeymoon," she laughed accepting her drink from him.

"It was pretty incredible," Jon replied. "I bought the yacht we rented."

"The one we all go on for July 4th and Memorial Day?" she

asked.

"It was over thirty years ago," he chuckled. "Nothing lasts that long."

"Well you never know," she raised her glass of champagne and proposed a toast. "To amazing honeymoons and healthy marriages."

"I'll drink to that," he said clinking his glass to hers and taking a sip. "Oh, that's good."

"Nearly icy, just how I love it," she teased. "You've spoiled me with expensive champagne."

"Champagne should be expensive," he answered. "I know we were going to talk about the case, but let's decompress for a moment, okay?"

Nodding, she set her champagne down and took the lid off her filet and garlic mashed potatoes.

"This looks delicious," she said taking her knife and cutting through the perfect medium rare.

"So, tell me, how's the wedding planning going?" Jon asked.

"Going well," she replied. "We're waiting to see if any of the venues we really want has one of the three dates available. Once we have that nailed down it'll be easy."

"And have you found the dress yet?" he asked.

"Mom and I are going again next weekend," she said. "I found a couple I liked but it wasn't quite it yet."

"As far as I know and I'm a guy so I don't know much about wedding dresses, but from what my female acquaintances have said, you'll know it as soon as you put it on."

"Yeah, I have pictures, wanna see?"

"Always," he replied. Pulling out her phone, she showed him the two she was interested in but after he saw them he nodded. "I agree with the second one but yeah I think there's something else needed."

"We have an appointment at this boutique. It's expensive but dad said he'll give me an extra two thousand toward the dress. They were already giving five and I have about three saved up. So that should be good so long as the consultant doesn't show me something I'll absolutely love that's like twelve thousand."

"And if it is," Jon said. "And it's the one, you tell me and I'll make up the difference. My nephew is getting married for the first and only time, Courtney. Don't even think of telling me no. And you know I love you so I want you to have the one you want."

"You are the sweetest person alive," she replied. "But I don't think I could."

"What did I just say?"

"I know I know, I'm frugal so sue me," she laughed. "You wanna help, buy us a house."

"Don't tempt me," Jon said.

"How about you? Wedding planning becoming your new favorite hobby?"

Jon laughed as he took a bite from his filet. "Beth is a dichotomy. One minute she wants the big white wedding and the next she wants a small intimate affair with just family and close friends," he said. "So we're kinda waiting until Scott and Kim have theirs in December and see."

"Yeah two weddings back to back," Courtney shook her head. "Our dates are mostly in March and May."

"Which one do you want?"

"Personally, March but I'm a little worried about St. Patrick's Day, I know we'll want to go over to Ireland."

"Don't be," Jon replied. "Your wedding is more important. I'm sure it'll work out."

"Oh, me too," she answered. "We're just waiting on the venue."

"Waiting can be the hardest thing," he said.

"I know," she laughed. "But now, maybe we should start talking about the case before this delicious champagne makes me tipsy."

Chapter
Twenty-Three

Brent sat in the black SUV across the street from the hotel.

He took feverish notes while listening intently to Jon and Courtney's conversation.

They were finally talking about Donna Cross, making plans to visit her sister's home the next day. Brent picked up his phone and dialed Meredith's number.

"Hey," he said when she answered. "They're not talking about anything important. Nothing we don't already know. And it sounds like they're going for a late night swim in the hot tub after they finish."

"Then you're going for a swim, too," she said.

"I can't," he lied. "I can't swim."

"Then what good are you? You know I don't like men who disappoint me, look what happened to Zach. I would hate to ruin your pretty face," she threatened.

"I'll see what I can do," he said.

"Good," she replied and hung up without another word.

Danny rolled over and answered the annoying buzzing of his phone. He had finally caught an hour of sleep until the phone rang waking him from his dreams. Clearing his throat, he answered.

"Yeah?" he said.

"Meet me at the pool and bring swim trunks," Brent's voice came from the other end.

"I just pulled a seventeen hour shift. Piss off."

Hanging up, Danny rolled onto his side and closed his eyes. After about five minutes, he heaved a sigh and ripped the sheets off him, cursing. Grabbing his swim trunks, he wrenched them on and took a t-shirt off the chair. Heading down the stairs to the pool, he saw Brent sitting there with a book.

"Why are we here?" he demanded.

"Someone woke up on the wrong side of the bed," Brent said.

"Piss off," he replied. "Now tell me what's going on."

"Jon and Courtney are coming down soon, they wanted a long soak in the hot tub," he explained. "Meredith wants us to listen in."

"Why didn't she bug the room then?" Danny asked. Brent shrugged.

"No clue, maybe she didn't want to risk it after the one Zach left, was found. I swear I've never seen a woman overreact so much as when the feed went dead".

"I'm not in the mood for your shenanigans," Danny replied. "I've got a splitting headache."

"Well it wasn't my idea to come here," he answered. "I think they want to give Meredith another chance to bug her room."

"They don't know about Meredith," Danny said.

"Yeah, I know," Brent replied. "But still."

"You're impossible," Danny answered. "I'm going for a swim."

Danny pulled off his shirt and slipped out of his flip-flops, hoping Brent didn't notice the tattoo on his left pectoral. Two dates in rather plain font were stacked on top of each other. Thankful he didn't say anything though he felt the man staring at him, Danny walked to the edge of the pool. They were not close enough friends to ask about that. Taking a deep breath, Danny dived in to the cold water.

It felt good on his overheated skin. The excursion of his tired muscles helped his mind stop thinking. He had been dreaming about his wife and daughter earlier and as much as the pain was still fresh after two years, he looked forward to the dreams, it was the only proof they lived. That and the Celtic knot necklace his Caitlin had given him on their sixth wedding anniversary. He wore it around his neck always remembering her beautiful red hair, the same hair their daughter had. Powering through the water, his lungs burned with the need for air but he ignored it. Any other pain would be better than the pain of loss.

⸻⸻∘❦∘⸻⸻

"This was an excellent idea," Courtney said as she relaxed against the side of the tub. Jon agreed and slipped in beside her, his eyes drifting to the man lounging beside the pool and the other powering through the water as if he were competing with Michael Phelps. He wondered why Steven had them there but then his words came back to him *don't be surprised if you see my two men following you. They are working for someone who wants you tailed.*

Courtney sighed and rolled her head over to look at him.

"Stop thinking for once," she said. "We know why."

"You being able to read my mind is just scary," Jon answered.

"I'm talented," she shrugged. "I was thinking though," she turned serious. "The plan is to go see Donna Cross's sister tomorrow, right?"

"Yes," Jon answered. "It would be best if we do it without telling anyone though."

"Good thing we have the address," Courtney said. "How are we going to do this?"

"I'm thinking we should play it safe," Jon replied. "We don't want to spook her."

"Agreed," Courtney wiped her hand across the water. "Do you think our new friends would be willing to work with us?"

152

"I wouldn't want to ask," Jon stated. "If there is someone else after us, I would rather have them tailing us than someone we can't trust."

"Do you trust them?" She asked.

"Steven does," Jon replied. "That's enough for me."

At that moment, Danny pulled himself out of the pool and grabbed his towel to dry off. Brent lifted the book he was reading so Jon could see the cover. Jon had to laugh when he read *Old Sins*, Beth's latest book.

"And I think they're listening and trying to tell me something," he said.

"Well, your voice carries," Courtney replied. "Everyone's voice carries in here."

"Good thing we're the only ones in here," Jon answered.

"You know," they heard Brent talking to Danny. "I really like how the author uses a deflective tactic, having her characters do one thing for the bad guy to think one way, all while acting and yet they know the ones that are following will also say and do something when they mean another."

"I don't understand what you're talking about," Danny sighed.

"Oh that's right you haven't read any of Elizabeth Nixon's books, huh? I forgot," Brent said. "You should. Especially this one. You know what they say; *old sins cast long shadows*. It's amazing how many people don't realize that."

"I'm not one of them," Danny answered. "I know my old

sins."

"Ooh scandalous," Brent replied.

"Most of them are back in Ole Ireland," Danny said. "It's amazing how one act can haunt you forever."

"Agreed or how one person can change your life," Brent replied.

"They're trying to tell you something," Courtney whispered.

Jon nodded but turned to her and wrapped his arm around her. His eyes told her everything she needed to know. With an almost imperceptible nod, she gave him permission. His lips brushed hers and her hands rubbed across his bare chest. They were using Brent's words about doing one thing and meaning another. It was an act for whoever they were reporting back to. Courtney broke his kiss and leaned her head on his shoulder.

"Tired?" he asked.

"A bit but not too tired for you," she admitted yawning.

"Good," he kissed her hair and helped her out of the hot tub. "You promised handcuffs if I drank your champagne."

"And you drank my champagne, someone's been naughty," she said as she wrapped the fluffy towel around her.

Jon pulled on his t-shirt and took her arm as they walked out of the room with a short backwards glance at Brent and Danny.

"Thank god they understood you," Danny said when he and Brent were alone. "I'm sure Meredith is very interested in hearing what we saw and heard."

"She is a jealous one that," Brent replied. "Still bitter about Jon's rejection nearly ten years ago."

"Women hold grudges," Danny answered. "But I think she's a little more upset about losing the Greene family fortune when Scott divorced her."

"Considering she got into bed with the lawyer who helped Scott, I think it shows she'd do anything to get her dues," Brent said.

"Tom Roberts, Rob, Paul Anderson he stoked the dying ember to life and threw petrol on it. She was off our radar before he showed up. Now the three heads would do anything for her."

"Some women have that effect on men. They're fascinated by her. Our job is to pretend to be and use whatever we can to take the three down."

"I hope Phoenix is all right," Danny said. "She's right in the middle of it all."

"Me too," Brent replied. "Me too."

Chapter
Twenty-Four

That next morning, Jon called Dave and put him on speaker while he and Courtney ate their breakfast. Giving their report on what happened the previous evening, leaving out meeting Steven and the other two agents, Dave ended the call by expecting them to report that evening and to return home as soon as possible.

When they hung up, Courtney looked over at Jon and shook her head.

"I don't think I've ever seen or heard Dave that upset," she said. "What do you think happened?"

"No clue," Jon replied. "He won't tell us."

"He can't be upset that we don't have much to report. And besides we can't report what we really know without endangering Steven's mission."

"True," Jon thought for a moment while he chewed his

scrambled eggs. "I wonder…"

"What?"

"Well, what if Steven is keeping him in the loop?"

"How and why would he do that? I mean, I know Dave is Homeland Security but they don't really communicate like that, pro bono," she said.

"Maybe there's more to this than we know. Remember when it comes to security, the police are at the bottom of the food chain."

"Yeah and I hate it," she answered eating a piece of bacon.

"Did you write down the address for the sister?" Jon asked.

"I did," Courtney jumped up and found her notepad. Flipping through it, she stopped on one page. "I wrote both addresses down just in case we wanted to go to see where Donna lives."

"Perfect," Jon drained his apple juice and stood. "I'm going to get dressed. Let's head out in twenty?"

"Sounds good," she answered. "I'll set up GPS on my phone to plug into your car."

"Great," Jon walked to his adjoining door and looked back. "You good?"

"Yeah, why wouldn't I be?" she asked.

"Just wanted to make sure," he answered. "I know it's been an… interesting trip."

"It definitely has," she agreed. "But now the case is moving forward and I'm not wasting half the day being a ball of emotion and half crazed woman with a gun."

Jon chuckled. "Well I'm glad you're over the ball of emotion part."

"Och, not funny," picking up a pillow she tossed it at him. Jon caught it and grinned.

"So I don't have to treat you any differently now?"

"Have you ever?"

"Touché," he answered. "Hurry up, I want to pick up some real coffee on the way."

Just as Jon was about to leave the room, his cell phone rang again. Pulling it out, he answered Dave's call.

"I looked up Donna Cross in our system, and ran a background check on her. She has a sister Karen."

"Yeah, we were hoping to visit her," Jon replied.

"She's an interesting character. She was divorced but the name has been redacted and secured. I got Callen here to get the original and I wanted to tell you what you're up against."

"Who is it?" Jon asked.

"How well do you know Senator Pellegrino?"

"Senator?" Courtney asked.

"Never heard of him," Jon replied.

"No no, the Senator is flirting with running for President next term. He's a powerful... though rather too forward thinking, figure in Washington. Is he related to Chief Pellegrino?" Courtney asked.

"His father actually," Dave replied. "Adam Pellegrino is the

Senator's son. The senator runs a charity that's been investigated. Opponents on the Hill think they're using charitable funds for personal use and gains. They might be right. There are numerous, shall we say payoffs out of the charity's account and coincidentally they coincide with Karen Pellegrino's many hospital visits."

"There's nothing I hate more than a corrupt wealthy Senator's abusive son," Jon said.

"Isn't it interesting he didn't mention he was brother-in-law to the victim," Courtney replied.

"Could be why he's been bugging our rooms," Jon said.

"Jon, this has to be dealt with delicately," Dave replied. "There's… a lot going on with this case. If I thought you would do it, I would pull you from it. But I know you won't so I need you to take care. Talk to the sister by all means, but don't involve the Chief. There was also a restraining order on him that got buried. Karen has been hiding from him for nearly ten years."

"Are there any children?"

"Two daughters," Dave answered.

"We need to go talk to Karen Cross," Courtney said looking at Jon.

"Do it, but be careful. This is bigger than you know," Dave replied and hung up.

"I knew he was far too accommodating. There was something he was trying to hide. He probably thought to wine and dine us, possibly sleep with you and we gave him the perfect blackmail material on us. He's probably gloating that he's going to get away with it," Jon said.

"Poor woman," Courtney replied. "She's probably scared to death she's next."

"Let's look on the brighter side, maybe she doesn't know and we can help her get away."

"Another relocation to Ireland?"

"If need be," he said. "By the way," he pulled out another phone he always carried with him. "I should talk to Greg," he said deliberately just in case someone was listening in. "About this. He might know something. I just find it odd an abusive husband isn't a dirty cop."

"You think he might be in with *him*?" She asked.

"No idea," he answered as he typed the text to Keelan. "But I'll find out as soon as he calls me." He sent the text. "Could be a shot in the dark. Might actually be worth checking out. Either way, at least all bases are covered."

<hr>

Keelan knocked on Viktor's door at two o'clock that afternoon but when he didn't answer, Keelan called his name. Opening the door, he saw Viktor's bed was made, as it was every morning and the curtains were opened. Suddenly worried, he went to the closet and breathed a sigh of relief when he saw his clothes still there. Just as he turned toward the door, he heard masculine laughter drift up from the entryway.

Walking to the stairs, he looked over the grand staircase and watched as Viktor and Iollan walked in. Iollan was dressed in his ridding outfit and Viktor wore jeans and a Polo with his new riding boots.

"Da'!" Iollan called up to him when he saw him. "Greg's a natural on a horse! You should've seen him. We took Lucky and Brida out. We even increased the pace to a full gallop. He did a grand job!" He slapped Greg on the shoulder.

"Of course," Keelan complimented heading down the stairs. "I'm glad you lads had fun."

"I'm famished," Iollan replied.

"I believe Kathleen has something laid out for you," Keelan answered. Iollan smiled and slapped his father's arm affectionately as he passed. Once they were alone, Viktor looked over at Keelan.

"Everything all right?" Viktor asked.

"Jon texted me. He was hoping we could call him after lunch?"

"Yeah, that'd be fine. Do you know what it's about?" Viktor asked.

"No," Keelan shook his head. "He just said that he had a question for you."

"Great," Viktor looked at his watch. "I'm about to digest my own internal organs. I need to eat then I'll call.

"You're around my son for too long, you're becoming as dramatic as he is," Keelan chuckled.

"Of course he is," Kathleen's voice came from the breakfast room. "Come in and eat before Iollan eats it all himself. And when you do speak with my son, tell him he needs to call his ma. Enough of this calling to just talk to you two," she teased. They followed her into the dining room and went to the side board to get their food.

Just as they sat down to their plates, the front doorbell rang. They waited to begin eating until O'Connell knocked on the door and walked over to Kathleen.

"Ma'am," he said in a somber tone. "Ms. Maighdhlin Lynch and the magistrate are here and have asked to speak with Mr. O'Grady."

Keelan went a little pale as all eyes turned to him, but eventually he took a deep breath and nodded. His sister-in-law came into the room followed by an older man with thinning white hair. Leaning back in his chair, Keelan locked eyes with Maighdhlin.

"I'm so sorry, Keelan," Maighdhlin whispered. Sighing, Keelan stood as the magistrate stepped forward.

"I'm sorry to do this, Mr. O'Grady, you and your family have been a great benefit to this county, this land and its people. I do not wish to cause you pain."

Keelan nodded once and squared his shoulders. "I appreciate your kind words, my lord, but please do not drag this out."

"I have here an envelope addressed to you," the old man went on and pulled out a legal envelop. "Please take it," he handed it to him. Once Keelan held the envelope, he went on. "You have received your wife's petition for dissolution of marriage, do you accept it?"

"No," Iollan breathed.

"I do," Keelan answered.

"Do you wish to contest the divorce?" He asked.

Keelan shook his head. "No, I do not," he replied.

"Da'!" Iollan cried.

Keelan closed his eyes for a moment, grateful Iollan could not see his face. No tears filled his eyes. He expected it. He was numb.

"I will have these signed shortly," he said.

"They have a caveat, you have seventy-two hours to sign and the request is you wait twenty-four," he replied.

"My wife's request?" he asked.

"No," he answered. "The courts'."

"Very well," Keelan answered.

"Da', please! Aunt Mags!" Iollan turned to his mother's younger sister.

"Your mother made her decision," she looked over at him with tears in her eyes. "Your father needs your support right now, Iollan." Keelan and Maighdhlin locked eyes for a moment before he looked away.

"I thank you for delivering these personally," Keelan said as if he had not heard his son's words. "O'Connell, please bring two extra plates," Keelan replied. "Please help yourselves to breakfast."

"Thank you but I should be going," the old man said.

"Of course," Keelan answered. "O'Connell?"

"I will see you out, sir," O'Connell stepped forward.

Maighdhlin watched her brother-in-law as Keelan looked down at the envelope in his hand, tapped it absently against his ring. He took a moment before he said anything, but finally he turned to Iollan and spoke softly.

"I'm sorry," he said. "I know this isn't something a son should have to experience but after your brothers' deaths there's nothing your mother or I could do. We cannot remain together the pain is too much. I pray you never experience the loss of a child, but do not look upon your mother any differently, lad. She's going through hell." Looking around the room, his eyes locked on Maighdhlin.

"I'm so sorry, Keelan," she said. "I tried to stop her. But—"

"She's a stubborn woman," he interrupted. "There's no point in pretending I did not see this coming. I hoped it wouldn't. I wish she'd let me speak to her. Once she makes her mind up that's what she sticks to," he cleared his throat and looked down. "Kathleen, please excuse me, I need to be alone."

"Of course," Kathleen said softly.

Keelan thanked her and left the room closing the door behind him.

"Maighdhlin, dear," Kathleen called when it looked like the younger woman would go after Keelan. "Come and sit."

She hesitated a moment then accepted the older woman's hand and sat beside her. "I don't think you have met Greg? He's a friend of Jonathan's. He's been staying with us."

"Yes, Keelan's mentioned you," she explained.

"I'm glad he has a friend like you, Maighdhlin," Kathleen went on. "Keelan needs all the love he can get right now."

"I don't understand," Iollan breathed. "How could ma do this?"

"She is going through hell, Iollan," Kathleen said.

"So is my da'!" he shouted.

"Iollan," Maighdhlin put a hand on his. "You know your ma is a wonderful woman but-"

"She is no'! You have been more of a mother to me than her, Aunt Maighdhlin," Iollan stood from the table and threw his napkin down. "And now she's done something unforgivable."

"God is our judge not you, son," Kathleen said.

"I'll judge whoever I damn well want to."

"Language," Kathleen snapped. Iollan had the presence of mind to look down ashamed. "Divorce is not something to take lightly, Iollan. Trust me. But it gives the wounded party a chance to heal. Have you forgotten I married Jon's father after he divorced his wife?"

"That is different," Iollan said.

"How so?"

"This is my life we're talking about," Iollan replied.

"And if your father were to move on?" Maighdhlin asked. "Or your mother? Would you deny them the chance to by happy?"

"The only one he should move on with is you, Aunt Maighdhlin," he replied ignoring his aunt's deep blush. "And as for that woman, I'll not have her anywhere near me nor my future family," Iollan stated. "It's well known she's sleeping around. My friend saw her coming out of another man's house."

"That does not mean anything," Maighdhlin said.

"It means everything," he replied. "And I will not have her near my children."

"You can't do that, Iollan, she is your mother!" Maighdhlin cried.

"She is nothing to me!" he shouted as he stalked out of the dining room and slammed the front door closed.

Chapter
Twenty-Five

Jon checked his watch as they came to a stop at a red light. Pulling out his phone to check, there was still no call from Keelan and his brows pulled together in concern.

"Still nothing?" Courtney asked.

"I don't know why," he said. "I'll give him another hour. Maybe he and Iollan are in town and he's not home at the moment."

"Iollan just graduated, right?" She asked.

"Trinity, last month," Jon answered. "But he went on a month long trip across Europe before coming home. He proposed to his girlfriend in Italy."

"Oh wow," she said. "And I thought Ireland was incredible. Did she say yes?"

"Of course," he replied. "They're setting a date soon."

"Four couples are getting married within months of each

other. This is going to be an expensive year," she laughed. "Maybe Ryan and I should elope."

"I don't think your parents or I would be all right with that," Jon stated.

"Nah, your right," she answered. "I've always dreamt of my big white wedding."

Jon's phone rang. "Finally," he sighed, pulled off the road and answered. "Jonathan Greene," he said.

"Sir, it's Vitya," he heard.

"Vitya, good to hear from you, is everything all right?" Jon asked.

"No, sir," he answered. "While we were at lunch, the magistrate and Keelan's sister-in-law came with divorce papers."

"Oh, dear god, no," Jon breathed.

"Everyone is very upset. Keelan needs to be alone and Iollan stormed out, we're trying to find him but we think he took his horse for a ride. I don't know what to do," he said.

"It's all right," Jon replied. "All you can do is be there for them, I can't. Please keep me posted on what happens, okay?"

"Okay," Viktor answered. "I just want to help them."

"I know you do," he comforted. "Trust me. But they need to go through this in their own time. The best thing you can do is just be there as a sounding board, a shoulder, or anything else they need."

After a short pause, Viktor cleared his throat and went on. "What did you need to talk to me about?"

"It doesn't seem to be important now," Jon replied. "But tell me, do you know if a man named Pellegrino ever worked with your father?"

"Senator Pellegrino?" Viktor asked. Jon looked at Courtney.

"Yeah," he prompted.

"He was one of Dad's corrupt senators," Viktor went one.

"One of?" Courtney replied.

"You don't really think D.C. is squeaky clean, do you?" He asked. "I saw him many times at our house and also Skyping with dad. His charity is a front for Dad's extra dirty money. The money he gets from lobbyists and other officials. No one can get anything on them. When there's a whiff of someone hearing something, Dad has them put down. You remember Langdon last year?"

"He was supposed to release something damning before the election," Courtney said.

"Yeah, ever wonder why his story was buried?" Viktor asked.

"He was buried six feet under?" Jon supplied.

"More like eighty feet under. He was given some cement shoes and dumped in Lake Michigan," Viktor said. "This is why I should be turning evidence over, Jon not stuck here while he's still at large."

"You need to stay put, Viktor," Courtney recognized the same tone of voice Jon used on Scott and Ryan from time to time.

"Yes, sir," Viktor answered softly.

"Listen, if you see Keelan, tell him I'm here if he needs to talk. We need to go," Jon said. "You promise me that you will stay where you are. No vigilante justice, okay? Swear it."

"I swear, Jon," he said.

"Good, trust me, Vitya, it will be all right." Jon hung up the phone and gripped the steering wheel tighter.

"Are you all right?" Courtney asked.

"No," Jon bit out. "That woman has been a thorn in his side from the beginning. I knew from the moment he told me she got pregnant she would always be a problem."

"Who?" Courtney asked.

"Aislín," Jon replied.

"Keelan's wife?"

"Aye, he was stupid and they got pregnant when they were eighteen. Even though I'm younger than he is, I knew she was playing him. Now she's chosen a moment when they're both hurting to yet again make it about her. Damn that woman."

"Whoa, I know you're pretty pissed at the moment and you have every right to be, he's your friend, but come on. I'm sure she has her reasons too."

"No," Jon stated. "He's been an amazing husband, father and friend. He doesn't deserve this. He even put his love for someone else on hold during these last few years they've been separated because he would not hurt her like that. But she's been screwing anything in pants for the past three years. He didn't care."

"Keelan's in love?" Courtney asked.

"And I hope he doesn't screw it up," Jon replied. "I know what it's like to be alone. I know how it is to mourn something but

Aislín doesn't deserve it. He needs to get his life back and if that means dating her sister then so be it."

"Whoa, hold on," Courtney said. Jon's shoulders fell as if deflated.

"Shit," he breathed. "I didn't mean for that to slip out. Forget it."

"Keelan is in love with his wife's sister?" Courtney asked.

"It's not like it's never been done," Jon replied. "Maighdhlin has always been there. Hell, she's been a better mother to his sons than his own wife. But neither of them will ever act on it. I just hope one of these days he won't regret the time lost." Jon's hands twisted around the steering wheel. After a moment, Courtney placed her hand on his knee.

"Hey, you and Beth have a lot of years left," she said. "Don't regret mourning Carol, okay?"

Nodding slowly, he breathed a laugh. "It's sometimes scary how well you know me."

"Reading minds was part of the job description I had to sign when Mat partnered us," Courtney teased.

Chapter
Twenty-Six

Jon and Courtney drove on in silence for the short drive out to one of Minneapolis' suburbs. Once the GPS told them they had arrived at Karen Cross's neighborhood, Courtney focused on the numbers of the house.

"There," she said seeing the correct address on the porch post of a small brown and white house. Jon put the car in park and removed his seat belt.

"Looks like someone is here," he said nodding toward the blue Prius in the driveway. "I don't know if Karen has been told of her sister's death and knowing what we do about her history with the police, she is likely to be a leery of strangers."

"Agreed," she said.

"You take lead. I don't know how she might react to me," he replied.

"I can do that," she answered.

After knocking and ringing the doorbell, the front door finally opened and a woman in her late thirties, who bore a striking resemblance to Donna Cross, looked at them expectantly.

"Yes?" She asked shifting the young girl in her arms to her other hip.

"Hi, Ms. Cross?" Courtney asked.

"Yes," she answered.

"My name is Courtney Shields and this is Jonathan Greene, we are actually from Indianapolis. We're detectives with the Indianapolis Metropolitan Police Department," they both pulled out their credentials. "We're currently investigating a case back east and we would like to speak with you about it, if we may."

"Is this about my father?" She asked.

"Yes, ma'am," Courtney replied. "We're very sorry for your loss."

She nodded and opened the door wider. "Please come in," she said.

Courtney headed in as Jon followed silently behind her.

"Please take a seat… if you can find one," she indicated the couch covered in the little girl's toys. Courtney sat on the edge of the couch as Jon stood beside her. Ms. Cross set the little girl down and told her to take her toys up to her room. Grabbing a couple, the four-year-old headed up the stairs. Once she was gone, Ms. Cross turned to Courtney. "It's a long drive for you to come all the way out here just to ask me a few questions. Can I get you something to drink?"

"No, thank you," Courtney replied pleasantly. Karen looked over at Jon who shook his head and smiled slightly.

"Are you working with the police here?" She asked taking a seat in an overstuffed chair across from the couch.

"We are, in so much as they have provided some key information regarding your father," Courtney said. "But we are conducting our own investigation."

"What can I help you with?" She asked. "Dad never talked about his cases, my sister and I don't have any idea what he was working on."

"Is your sister here?" Courtney asked.

"No, she left on a trip a couple days ago," she said.

"We believe your father may have been killed due to a case he was presiding over," Courtney went on. "I know you mentioned he never talked about his cases but did he mention anything at all about the most recent case?"

"No," she replied. "Dad was old school. But why come all the way out here? You could have easily called me."

"We did, ma'am but there was no answer. My partner did leave a message."

"I never got a call," she answered looking up at Jon.

"Perhaps we had an older number. Have you been informed of another possible incident related to your family, Ms. Cross?" Courtney proceeded delicately.

"What possible incident?" She asked.

"Something to do with your sister, maybe?" She asked.

"What are you talking about?"

"Ms. Cross, what I have to say is going to be difficult," Courtney said. "We have reason to believe your father was coerced into allowing a very dangerous man off."

"Coerced how?" She asked. "Dad was as straight-laced as they come."

"We're afraid the man whose trial he was hearing was a known mobster," Courtney went on. "He had connections here and it looks like your sister was kidnapped and held hostage until your father released him."

"What?" She breathed. "No, that's not possible. Where is she? Is she safe?"

"Ms. Cross, I'm sorry to be the one to tell you this, but she was found on the steps of the courthouse in Minneapolis three days ago. I am afraid she was killed," Courtney said.

Karen locked eyes with Courtney and held her gaze.

"I just spoke to her Monday," she said. "She was looking forward to her trip… my god, three days? Why hasn't anyone come and told me?"

"I believe they didn't know you were staying here," Courtney replied.

"This is my home of course I'm staying here," she said. "How was she identified?"

"There was no ID on the body but her credit card was. We are still waiting on a formal identification," Courtney answered.

"Her prints were not in the system so it's taking a little longer with dentals."

"How was she killed?"

"She was shot, Ms. Cross," she said.

Karen closed her eyes for a moment. "Did she suffer?" She asked.

"We do not think so, it would have been quick," she said.

"Did he... did he rape her?" She asked.

"There was no sign of sexual assault," Courtney replied.

"Oh, thank god," she let out. "Oh god, her kids... who's going to tell them?"

Courtney looked back at Jon. "We had no idea Donna had children," she said.

Karen looked at her sharply. "What are you talking about?" she asked.

"There was no record of Donna Cross having children," she said again.

"Is this some kind of sick joke?" she demanded.

"Ms. Cross?" Courtney questioned surprised.

"Who are you? Did he send you?" She got up.

"Ms. Cross, please," she replied.

"No, no you tell me," she said.

"We're following up on information about your sister, Donna's death," Courtney said.

"*I'm* Donna Cross," she replied.

"What?" Jon asked.

"Who are you?" Donna questioned. Jon and Courtney looked at her stunned. "Who are you?" She demanded.

"Ms. Cross," Jon said pulling out his phone. "I'm sorry to have to show you this, but is this your sister?"

He showed her a picture of the woman in the morgue. Donna let out a cry as she looked at the picture.

"That son of a bitch." She sank back down into her chair.

"Ms. Cross," Jon asked again.

"He's finally done it," she said as tears filled her eyes. "He's finally killed her."

"Is that your sister?" Courtney asked.

"Yes, that's Karen," she answered.

"I'm very sorry," Courtney said. "And I am sorry for the confusion. We thought you were Karen and she was Donna."

She stood and went to the end table where her purse sat. Jon tensed for a moment wary of what she was doing. When she pulled out her billfold, he relaxed. "Here's my driver's license. She must have had... of course, she went shopping for the girls three days ago, she took my credit card. It has my name on it."

"You said *he* finally did it, who is he?" Jon asked.

"Her ex-husband," she replied.

"Chief Pellegrino?" Courtney asked.

"You know him?" She asked.

"We met," she replied. "We couldn't come to his town without it."

"*His town* all right," Donna said. "Very apt description.

God, I told Karen not to get involved with him."

"How long have they been divorced?" Jon asked.

"Ten years," she replied.

"And that little girl you were holding, is she yours or Karen's?" Jon asked.

"What does that have to do with anything?" She asked sharply.

"If she is your sister's we need to know who the father is," Jon said.

"It's none of your business," she replied.

"Please, Ms. Cross," Courtney said. "I can vouch for my partner. He would not ask if he did not think the child could be important."

Donna looked from one to the other of them and sighed.

"She's Karen's," she said. "Karen had an affair with Adam Pellegrino's brother; Curtis. She and Curtis knew each other from school, they were dating for a while but Curtis fell into the wrong crowd and he was arrested a couple times. He wasn't someone our father wanted her to be with. That is when Adam came home, Mr. Ivy League, secure career, daddy's boy but who would beat the living shit out of her if she didn't iron his shirt right or if she cooked something for dinner he didn't want. Of course, I wanted her to go to the police, but every time, her case would be conveniently misplaced and he would come home and do it all over again. It's a miracle he didn't kill her. They had been divorced for several years when Curtis got out of prison and came back into her life. But Adam would have known it was Karen, not me."

"Your father actually said your name before he died," Jon replied. "That, partnered with your credit card found on her body everyone naturally assumed it was you."

"And he just went along with it," she finished his thought. "Ever since he found out about them, he has wanted them both dead. You said this guy Dad let off has ties to the mob and here?" They nodded. "Can I ask, is it the Russian Mob?"

"Why do you think that?" Jon prodded.

"Because there was a big takedown just a couple weeks ago of a gambling den laundering money for a branch of the Russian mob," she said. "It wouldn't surprise me if Adam got a little idea in his head."

"Ms. Cross, does the name Viktor Redorvsky mean anything to you?" Courtney asked.

"Viktor *Demetrovich* Redorvsky?" She asked.

"Yes," Jon answered.

She looked at them and then turned to the hutch under the window. She unlocked it and pulled out a large file.

"I may not have told the whole truth when I said my father didn't talk about his cases. It's true he didn't normally, but on occasion he would if he felt his life could be in danger. About a month ago, Karen and I received this in the mail with strict instructions from him to keep it under lock and key and not give it to anyone around here. He said if he died there may be someone coming to look for it, and if I felt they were honest, I was to give it to them. I think you should see it," she said handing the file to Jon.

"Case notes, courtroom minutes, photos, all of this is evidence," Jon said as he flipped through it. "How did he get copies?"

"I don't know. When we asked him, he said it would be safer if we didn't know... It didn't help Karen though," she went back to the couch and sat down next to Courtney.

"Is there someone we can call to come and be with you?" Courtney asked.

"My mother's sister is in Duluth, I'll give her a call," she replied. "I don't want to stay here now."

"Of course," Courtney stood and pulled out a card. "If you have any questions or if you think of anything else, please don't hesitate to call us."

"Thank you," she said.

Just as she accepted it, the window glass shattered and gun fire rang out. Courtney grabbed Donna and dove to the floor. They both covered their heads as wood and plaster splintered around them. When the shots ended, Jon got up and ran to the front door.

"Cover me," he yelled. Courtney didn't think as she fired her gun. Car doors slammed and tires squealed. After a moment, Jon came back inside. "Are you all right?"

She nodded but put her gun away and balled her fists so Donna couldn't see her hands shaking.

"Ms. Cross?" She asked.

"I'm fine," she answered then they heard a young child's

shrill cry from upstairs. "Chloe!" She screamed and ran upstairs where her niece was playing. Courtney looked at Jon. Her breathing picked up and her body shook. Jon placed his hands on her shoulders and forced her to look at him. They said nothing for a while

Donna came down the stairs clutching her niece to her. The little girl cried into her aunt's shoulder.

"What the hell was that about?" Donna hissed.

"I think they wanted the file," Jon replied. Sirens blared in the distance and Jon looked at Courtney then Donna. "Ms. Cross, we need to leave. If the chief finds out we were here it could destroy what little hope we have of getting this," he held up the file, "into the right hands. Will you promise to not let them know we were here?"

"I'll not mention it," she swore. "But how am I going to explain this?" She looked at the side of the house that was nearly gone.

"Tell them the truth, just leave us out of it," Courtney replied.

"Okay," she answered. "Promise me you will get the man who ruined my little sister's life."

"We will," Jon said.

"We should go," Courtney coaxed hearing the sirens coming closer. Jon tossed her the car keys.

"You drive," he said. "I need to make a call."

<hr />

Brent held his gun down by his thigh as he sat in the van across from the house. The Irish Mob was getting bold to attack in broad daylight in a suburb. His finger twitched to the trigger but he stayed his hand. Jon and Courtney walked out and he flashed his lights at them. Looking down the street, they crossed to his car as he rolled the window down.

"Who the hell was that?" Jon demanded.

"Eammon O'Malley," he answered.

"Who?" Courtney asked.

"The head of the Irish Mob here in the states," Brent said.

Courtney looked over at Jon, his face was pale and his hands were clenched into fists.

"Jon?" She asked placing a hand on his arm. She drew back when she felt the tension in his forearm.

"What the hell is he doing here?" Jon demanded through clenched teeth. "He's in New York."

"He's been here for a couple years now," Brent stated. "Look, I can't be seen talking to you. If all goes well, I'll come to your rooms tonight and answer your questions, but right now, I need to go."

"Wait," Jon stopped him from rolling up the window. "Just tell me, does he know I'm here?"

"No," Brent replied. "It's not you he's after. But like Steven said, we have agents in the field that may die if you don't drop this."

Without another word, Brent rolled up his window and drove off. Courtney placed her hand on Jon's arm again, the tension still there but not nearly as much.

"Jon?" she asked.

"You know the saying, Courtney?" he started still looking after Brent's car.

"What saying?"

"Old sins cast long shadows," he replied. "Some old sins are better left undisturbed."

"Riley said that name before he died," she pressed. "You need to level with me, partner. What's going on?"

Finally, Jon turned to her, his face emotionless. "I'm a dead man."

Chapter
Twenty-Seven

"Uh… what do you mean you're a dead man?" Courtney demanded. "Who the hell is Eammon O'Malley?"

"Let's go back to the hotel. I need a drink and I'll tell you everything," he promised.

———◦———

Once they were back at the hotel, Jon went to the bar and asked for a bottle of whiskey. Taking the bottle up to Courtney's room, they sat in the two chairs by the window, the curtains drawn. Jon poured the whiskey in two glasses, a little more for him, then handed Courtney the glass. She sipped it and watched Jon as he took a gulp. His hand still shook and the color hadn't returned to his lips. Once he took a drink, he closed his eyes and let out a shuttered breath. She had never seen him so scared. Before he spoke, he took a second drink, finishing the whiskey in his glass. Pouring another, smaller amount, he held the glass, not drinking yet.

Finally, he began, but did not raise his eyes to her.

"Do you remember when we had Quinn Henderson in custody a couple months ago?"

"Yes," she answered.

"Do you remember the story I told you about May 20, 1968?"

"Belfast and the IRA?"

"Yes," he replied taking a drink.

"I remember you told me the story about your friend; Jimmy?"

"Yeah," he answered softly. "What I didn't tell you is, the man who was our commander of sorts, was the nephew of a well-known anarchist who led the Irish Mob in New York. The man we worked for had ambitions and the only way to get his uncle's attention was to make some noise in Ireland for the cause. He made the bomb without a kill switch so it would have to go off no matter what. When Jimmy was killed he figured out why, meaning we shirked our duty to let the school blow up. None of us used our real names but he knew who I was.

"He found me in New York, I was lucky to survive his gang of attackers, never getting his hands dirty of course. My best friend, my godson Jason's father, found me half dead and got me to the hospital. My ma and da' filed a police report but I didn't tell them anything. I couldn't. I remember vividly what he said to me, 'I will destroy your family, if you so much as breathe a word of this to anyone, they're dead.' I thought he gave up when I went to Vietnam, but he showed up again outside my flat with pictures of me and Beth. He told me if I didn't help him, he would kill her. I was on his *payroll* for a little over six months. Anything he needed done, I would be the one. He always knew of my sniper training and... well that's a part of me I've buried.

"When da' died, ma moved back to Ireland and I moved to Texas to be with Carol, I didn't hear from him again but I've always looked over my shoulder. For the longest time, I thought he was the one behind Carol's death but when it was Paul... I was relieved. I've eluded him for thirty plus years and now..." his hand shook again when he raised the glass to his lips. "If anything happens to you or anyone I love, I will never forgive myself."

"You're petrified of him," Courtney surmised. Jon locked eyes with her.

"Yes," he answered simply.

"He's just one man," she said.

"One man with a long reach," he replied.

"Brent said he didn't know you were here," she said.

"It's only a matter of time," he answered. "If he's working with Pellegrino he'll know soon."

"Then we go home and let Steven take care of it," she said. "We can't fight this. It's not cowardice to run sometimes."

Jon said nothing for a moment, taking another drink from his whiskey.

"Let's get the file to the DA back in Indiana and speak with Adam Pellegrino once more before we leave. We need to know why he didn't tell us the truth."

"We know why he didn't tell us the truth," she answered. "He's working with the Russian mob using his ex-wife as collateral against his former father-in-law in order to get a known killer off."

"He needs to know the jig is up," Jon replied successfully finishing the whiskey in his glass. "Let's go talk to him. Then I want to see about meeting Brent here later tonight."

They were shown into the chief's office almost immediately. Surprised that Kyle Harris wasn't there, Jon and Courtney stood before the desk and waited.

"Lieutenant Greene and Detective Shields," Pellegrino said standing and offering his hand. Gesturing to the chairs behind them, Pellegrino sat in his desk chair and spoke again. "I understand you drove out to see Karen Cross today."

"Yes," Jon answered.

"Is she well?" he asked.

"I am curious if it was you who hired the hit on her," Courtney stated coolly. "There were enough bullets fired to tear down one of her walls."

"What?" He demanded suddenly scared. "Is she okay? What about Chloe? Is she all right?"

"How long have you known it is your ex-wife, Karen who is

down in the morgue and not Donna?" Jon asked.

"Karen? No no, Donna is in the morgue. It's Donna who is dead not my Karen," he replied.

"Bold words from a man who beat the shit out of his wife whenever he damn well pleased," Courtney answered. "There's one thing I cannot stand and that's wife beaters."

"Wife beaters and cops who use their power to make any little thing they don't like, go away," Jon added.

"Lieutenant, tell me the truth! Is Karen all right?" The man was on the verge of fainting.

"No, but then you knew that. That's why you had Eammon O'Malley's men follow us to Donna's house earlier today."

"Eammon who? What? No, I had nothing to do with that. I love Karen," fumbling, he pressed the button on the speaker and barked. "Harris, get in here."

When the door opened, Kyle Harris stood before them in his usual suit. His eyes flittered to Courtney then back to the chief.

"You called chief?" he asked.

"Did you know?" he demanded.

"Know what, sir?"

"Drop the act, Harris, this isn't funny anymore," the chief shouted. "Did you know Adam had Karen killed?"

Harris's eyes grew wide for a moment then shifted between Jon and Courtney.

"Answer me, dammit!" he yelled.

"Maybe you should sit down, sir," Harris replied walking

over to him and taking his arm. "I'm sorry, Lieutenant, Detective, he's a little overworked. Could you give us a moment?"

"What is going on?" Jon didn't budge.

"Chloe? Is Chloe all right?" the chief clutched at Harris's arm as the PR manager unbuttoned his collar and loosened his tie. "Please tell me you didn't have anything to do with this, Kyle. Dear god we trusted you."

"And I've never given you a reason to doubt my trust," Harris replied. "But this is not a conversation to be having right now."

"They already know," Pellegrino said.

"Not all of it," Jon stated.

"How long have you and your brother been switching places, Curtis?" Courtney asked. Jon looked over at her, then understanding dawned on him.

"Adam held my previous life over me. He demanded I take his place for things he considered too beneath him or boring to deal with. We are identical twins," Pellegrino said. "It was for image, nothing more. Karen and I were going to run away together. Kyle tell them!"

Kyle looked between the two of them, then nodded.

"I warned you to stay away from Adam, Detective," he said. "I said he wasn't a good man."

"We need to talk," Jon replied.

"Is my daughter all right?" Curtis asked.

"She's fine and with her aunt," Jon answered.

Visible relief shown on his face. "Kyle please, send someone to protect them, just until I can be there myself."

"Yes," Kyle promised. "I will see to it. But you need to relax, remember your heart."

"I don't give a damn," Curtis said. "Just take care of my daughter." Kyle nodded and looked over at Jon and Courtney. Without another word, he left the room.

"I apologize for the deception," Curtis spoke low. "I don't know how much of my past you know, but I was the black sheep and my father kept me hidden from public eye. When my brother approached me to take his place on things he thought too beneath him, I thought it was his way of accepting me back. But I was a means to an end. If I would refuse, he would use my past and Karen against me. My brother has used me for the last time."

Just as he said those words, the window splintered and he flinched twice. Looking down, blood spilled out of his chest. Jon and Courtney hit the floor as soon as the glass shattered.

"Courtney, stay with him!" Jon yelled, his gun already in hand. Looking across to the building opposite, a glint of a rifle caught his attention. He ran for the door, dodging two rounds.

"My daughter," Curtis gasped when Courtney reached him. "Please take care of my daughter."

"Officer down!" Courtney shouted.

"I'm not an officer," he gasped.

"I need some help in here!" She yelled ignoring Curtis's words.

"Please, don't let Adam near Chloe. She means everything to me," he said.

"Shh," Courtney soothed.

"He killed Karen because of us. Don't let him kill my daughter."

"Who?" Courtney pressed. "Who did this?"

"Adam… Adam is a marksman," he said. "He did this. He told me…"

"What, tell me, Curtis, please," she begged.

"He told me… Meredith," he gasped. "Meredith… she's calling the shots this time. He's working with two others. Please save my child."

"I will," she promised. "But you will be fine. She will want her daddy."

"Please, tell her I love her," he said.

"I will," she replied. "I promise."

He passed out just as the EMTs rushed into the room.

Chapter
Twenty-Eight

"Courtney!" She heard behind her.

Turning, "Jon!" she cried. "Oh, thank god!" she met him halfway in the waiting room of the hospital. "You didn't answer your phone. Never do that to me again."

He pulled out the black device and showed the shattered screen. "Sorry, wasn't intentional."

"Are you all right?" she asked seeing his arm held tightly at his side and a red bump on his forehead.

Not answering her, he changed the subject. "How is he?"

"Still in surgery," she said. "Doctors aren't sure. What happened?" she asked.

"I got in the building across the street. It was abandoned. Found the room but had to dodge a bullet myself. Landed on my shoulder wrong."

"Your shoulder?" she asked concerned, her hand ghosting across the joint.

"Yeah, dislocated it," he answered.

"Okay, let's get you checked in and get that taken care of," she said.

"No, I'm fine," he replied. "We don't have time anyway. I just need a good wall and some medicine."

"You are not forcing it back in yourself," she stated. "Now come with me."

"I'm fine," he denied. "Hardened war vet here, Courtney. I've had a dislocated shoulder before. But I could use a sling. I saw a Walgreens on the way here."

"You are getting checked out and that's final," she crossed her arms over her chest and Jon had to consciously stop his laugh.

"Fine, I know better than to cross a mama bear. Lead the way," he teased.

Once Jon was checked in and escorted to a room, the male nurse helped him take off his button-up shirt and handed it to Courtney. His undershirt was another issue, the nurse did not want to move Jon's shoulder any more than necessary and proceeded to cut the fabric away. Courtney gasped softly when she saw the reddening joint.

"I'm fine," he encouraged. "It hardly hurts."

"The doctor will be in shortly, but I'll go ahead and send in all the paperwork," the nurse said.

Once he was properly checked in, Courtney sat beside his

bed. He shivered and winced.

"Those idiots took your shirt and left you without any covering," she mumbled, stood and searched for a blanket.

"I'm fine, honestly," Jon replied wincing again as he adjusted in the bed.

"Jon, your shoulder is dislocated. You have a knot on your forehead. Do not tell me you're okay. If it were me what would you be doing?"

"That's different."

"No, it's not and to say it is, is misogynistic," she argued.

Rolling his eyes, he huffed. "I'm old school, sue me."

"Ah ha!" she cried eureka when she found a folded blanket. Placing it over him, she framed his face and forced him to look at her. "I care about you, okay? I love that you would take care of me, but let me do the same, okay?"

"Ryan is damn lucky," he replied. "I forgot how it was having someone fuss over me. I haven't needed it in a long time."

She didn't answer for a moment but finally leaned forward and kissed his cheek. "From Beth," she whispered.

"Thank her for me," he said just as the doctor walked in.

———◦◦———

Fully outfitted with a sling and some medicine to help the swelling after the doctor worked the joint back into place, Jon checked himself out and they returned to their hotel. As soon as they entered, Brent Tyler stood from Jon's chair.

"What the hell happened to you?" he demanded.

"Tell us what's going on with Curtis and Adam Pellegrino," Jon answered.

Courtney maneuvered Jon to the bed and helped him sit with his back against the headboard.

"First tell me what happened," Brent said. Jon leaned his head back and nodded to Courtney. She first poured him a glass of water and then, sitting beside him, she started telling Brent what had happened since they talked at Donna's house earlier that day.

"Damn, Steven's not going to like this," he breathed when she finished.

"Did you know he had Curtis cover for him?" Courtney asked.

"We had suspicions but weren't sure," he revealed.

"Who is Adam Pellegrino?" Jon asked.

"He's the head of the Italian mob here in the Midwest. We believe he's working with Redorvsky and O'Malley. They're planning something. Something big."

"What?" Jon asked.

"We don't know, that's what one of our own has gone undercover to discover," he explained. "This association has been years in the making. Bringing together three of the most powerful families in the States and using their connections. Of course, Al Qaeda is offering to make up a fourth and that's where Steven comes in."

"What about you?" Jon asked.

"I'm not CIA but I'm working with them stateside."

"Who do you work for?" Courtney asked.

"Another security firm. Don't ask, I wouldn't be able to tell you. Our team found out Pellegrino is working with a woman who is hell bent on seeing you destroyed. She worked with Paul Anderson a couple months ago. It looks like she's upped her game. Steven knew you would need someone watching your back."

"What woman?" Jon asked. "What's her name?"

"She is very dangerous. Among many motives the one she has revealed to us is she's seeking revenge on you for killing Paul Anderson," Brent said.

"I want a name," Jon replied.

"Meredith," he said. "Meredith Ventmore."

"Curtis said that name before he passed out," Courtney stated.

"Scott's ex-wife," Jon replied.

"She has been working with Adam Pellegrino for about a month. Ever since Paul Anderson was killed," Brent replied.

"Paul mentioned he still had a queen left to play," Courtney said.

"What is the play?" Jon asked.

"She is using Pellegrino to get in bed with the Russians," Brent said. "Pellegrino wanted his wife dead so when they formed an alliance, the first act of good faith, if you will, was for Pellegrino to help get Redorvsky out of prison. Kidnapping his ex-wife gave them the leverage they needed and Pellegrino got what he wanted.

Everyone was happy. Now the Irish are involved and they are using Pellegrino's pull with the police force to help fuel their trafficking."

"Who is the leader behind all this?" Jon asked. "Who is in the center of the web? I don't think Meredith is capable of doing all of that."

"We think there is another," Brent went on. "But that is what our agent on the inside is trying to find out."

Courtney's phone rang. Standing, she went into the bathroom to answer it.

"This goes a lot further than a domestic dispute with your son and his ex," Brent replied. "Steven told us everything."

"Then you know Paul Anderson alias Tom Roberts alias Rob was my son's dear friend and the lawyer who represented him at the divorce trial. He was also Steven's father and my fiancée's ex-husband," Jon said.

"Which was why he was going after you," Brent said. "And why Meredith is so intent on bringing you down. She's gotten in bed with all three leaders and is playing each one to her will."

"She was always good at that," Jon answered.

Courtney came back out of the bathroom, tapping her phone against her palm. "Curtis Pellegrino didn't make it," she said. "He died fifteen minutes ago in the OR."

"This just turned into a murder investigation," Jon replied. "You have everything well in hand, Brent. Courtney and I are going after Meredith and Adam."

"No, you do that and my partner could die. She is

undercover. Everything has been planned. You do something to mess it up and she will die. I honestly think it would be best if you both went back to Indy," he said. "Meredith and Adam will go wherever you are. If we can get them away from O'Malley one part of the wall will crumble. It's a tenuous relationship to begin with."

"Then we'll go back," Jon said. "Tell me, is Steven still stateside?"

"I am afraid I cannot answer that," Brent said. "But here is a number you can call if you need to get a hold of us. We will not answer but leave a message and say the word *Skylark* if it's an emergency."

"Thank you," Jon took the number, programmed it into his phone, and handed it back. Brent lit a match and burned it.

"Be careful," Brent said as he headed to the door.

"You as well," Jon answered. "Tell Steven to call me when and if he can."

Chapter
Twenty-Nine

Keelan tried to ignore the knock at the door. He didn't want to talk. His mind was still processing the divorce papers. Iollan had tried to come in earlier but Keelan asked him to leave him be for a little bit. Kathleen had tried to talk with him but he begged her to go to his son knowing Iollan could use her motherly approach. Now the only person left to knock on his door was Viktor and he knew he needed to assure him everything was all right.

"Come in," Keelan sighed.

The door opened and Viktor stood in the doorway, a tray in his hands.

"I don't want to bother you. I know what it's like to want to be alone, but... you've been so kind to me. I just wanted to say thanks and I thought you might be hungry," Viktor said.

Keelan smiled slightly. "Thank you, I am," he replied.

"I only know how to make American and Russian. Viktor set the tray down on the bed. "We didn't have any ingredients for Russian so I thought... nothing comforts me more than a bacon cheeseburger with chips and I thought you might want a beer," Viktor took the lid off the plate to show what he had cooked. It looked and smelled amazing.

"Looks greasy and completely bad for me... just the way I like it," Keelan said. "Thank you."

"I know it's not much, but I wanted to do something," Viktor replied.

"And it means a lot," Keelan answered. "Thank you. Where's Iollan?"

"He went out earlier. I think he went out for a ride," Viktor said.

"I'm thinking about going out on one meself," Keelan said.

"Please be careful," Viktor asked. "I never... I never had a dad and you and Jon are two men I am lucky to know. I've grown to love both of you as a father."

"I promise I will be," Keelan swore. "Now go, I'm all right, lad."

"Enjoy," he shrugged and walked out of the room.

———◦◦◦———

Zoe walked down the hallway, her finger rimming the bottom of her champagne glass. Voices came from the kitchen, stopping just short, she listened.

"I don't care what you have to do, you get that slut out of here," a man's voice she had never heard spoke heatedly.

"Just because they know about your little scheme, doesn't mean they know about me. And that slut, as you say, stays." Eammon said.

"She must be damn good if you're willing to ruin this whole thing. It took me years to get this planned, dammit!"

"She doesn't know anything," Eammon stated. "And I'm not ruining anything. Now I need you to get in touch with Redorvsky and make sure he hasn't messed up your plan worse than you have."

"You—"

"Your little stunt nearly bolloxed the whole plan," Eammon retorted. "Jaysus, you little twit, you're lucky I don't stop this whole thing!"

"I am not the one who invited a stranger into my bed. Have you revealed anything, Eammon? Pillow talk, maybe?"

"Unlike you, I have more restraint," he said. "Now why don't we go back out and rejoin the party?"

"I hope you know what you're doing…"

"Katie," Zoe whipped around at the sound of her alias. "What are you doing here?" One of the women guests at the part gushed. "We've been looking for you."

"Sorry, Mona, guess I got lost on the way out of the little girl's room." She covered and hoping against hope the men didn't hear.

"Oh, I know, this is such a big house!" Mona gushed as Katie took a gulp of her champagne and walked away quickly.

Chapter Thirty

"All right, Dave what have you got?" Jon asked when Courtney put her phone on speaker. They had decided to call their captain early that morning and explain everything. Dave took the news of them encroaching on a CIA op rather well, they thought; only cursing once and finally agreeing to help them research Adam and Curtis Pellegrino. He called back two hours later.

"Adam Pellegrino does have a twin brother. Petty criminal in his teens, did about five years for armed robbery. His US Senator father and a rising star in the police force brother didn't want the publicity so they kept it hush-hush."

"But I need to speak with you off the record."

"Oh?" Jon asked.

"As I was researching for you, I received a very interesting email and I think you need to hear it."

"Who's it from?" Courtney asked.

"Steven," Dave stated. Jon and Courtney looked at each other.

"Is he trying to recruit you and Homeland to help him?" Jon asked.

"You could say that," Dave sighed. "Look, there's more to this than we even know. I need you back here ASAP. It's not just a homicide anymore. I'm pulling the plug."

"You have got to be kidding," Courtney said.

"I'm serious, Courtney," Dave replied. "Look, I know you two, you're tenacious, but you have to know there are agents in the field who could be hurt or killed if you say the wrong thing."

"Dave, tell me, are you asking us to do this because you think it's for the best interest of all involved?" Jon asked. "I don't think my future stepson would recruit you if it's not important."

"You're right," Dave said. "And to answer your question, yes. I think it's best. He's laid it out, broke protocol to tell me, but I can't risk what he says is at stake."

"But Dave—"

"Courtney, I've never asked you to stop. In fact, other than your parents and Jon I've been the one to encourage you in your pursuits so I need to ask you a question... Do you trust me?"

"That's not fair," she countered. "You know I trust you in all things, but I can't overlook the fact a man is dead and it's my job to protect, defend and to find the person responsible."

"And that is what I love about you. If I had a daughter I

would hope she would be just like you. I know Jon believes the same. But right now, there's an old adage that says, choose your battles. I know about Jon's shoulder and the death of the chief, or rather his twin. It seems to me you both have caused quiet the stir over there. I would feel better if you were here. On neutral territory. Please, Courtney."

It took her a second but she sighed and nodded. "Okay," she said. "We'll close out here and be home soon."

They hung up and looked at each other. "If we're going to be driving ten hours I'm going to need to catch up on my sleep. My shoulder's aching and the medicine is affecting me. I didn't sleep well last night," Jon said.

"Are you okay?" Courtney immediately jumped up to help him.

"I'm fine," he replied. "Nothing a good rest won't cure."

"You rest then, I'm going to shower and call Ryan."

He nodded and she went to her room shutting the adjoining door behind her to give him some peace as he slept.

Courtney pulled off her blouse and threw it on the chair. Walking to her bathroom she turned on the shower. As she waited for the water to fill for a bath, she pulled off the rest of her clothes and left them in a pile on the floor. Pinning her medium length hair up off her neck, she stepped in and slipped under the water. It soaked into her sore muscles relieving the tension from the day. She reached over to her phone and called her fiancé.

About an hour later, she turned the water on again to wash

her hair and rinse off. After drying, she wrapped the towel around herself, opened the bathroom door and froze. Her entire room had been ransacked. Her clothes were ripped out of her suitcase and thrown around the room, the sheets of the bed pulled off. She started forward and as soon as she reached the foot of the bed, she saw movement to her right then pain radiated at the back of her head.

Everything went black.

Zoe stroked the greying hairs on Eammon O'Malley's chest as they lay together. Hoping to distract him after Mona had called her name as she stood outside the door, Zoe pulled out all the stops in her seduction. But as they lay together, she wasn't convinced it worked.

"What did you hear?" He asked and she tried not to freeze.

"When?" She questioned kissing his shoulder.

"Don't play coy," he gripped her hair so tightly she winced when he forced her to look at him.

"I'm sorry," she replied. "I was looking for you and I heard voices. Mona called me away. I heard something about saying something to a stranger but that's it."

He locked eyes with her and slowly nodded. "Good." He rolled them both and hovered over her kissing her neck successfully distracted from the blunder.

Chapter Thirty-One

"Courtney?" Jon sat up in bed. Something had woken him coming from Courtney's room. Removing the sheets, he stood too quickly and fell back down. The pain meds the hospital had given him were powerful but the pain in his shoulder took his breath away. Blinking hard to rid his sight of the black spots, he stood again, slower.

"Courtney?" he called again. When he didn't hear a response, he went over to the adjoining door and knocked.

"Courtney?" When she still didn't answer him, he tried to push the door open. It was shut fully. He knocked loudly. "Courtney!" he called and grabbed his phone to called her. He heard his ringtone play on her phone through the door but there was no answer. He knocked again. "Courtney!" He shouted.

He rushed to his wallet to get her spare key, but the key was gone. Without a second thought, he left his room and went to front door, banging and calling her name. Using his good shoulder, he tried to force the door but it wouldn't budge.

Then another door opened and a hotel maid left one of the other rooms.

"Help me, please," he called out to her. "My partner is not responding, I think something is wrong." He fumbled to show his badge. She blinked. "Please," he said. "She could be hurt."

She finally nodded and took out her master key card. Once the door was unlocked, Jon ran in and froze. Not only was the room ransacked but Courtney lay face down on the carpet wrapped in a hotel towel. He slid over to her on his knees, ignoring the gasp of the woman behind him.

"Call an ambulance!" he cried. She disappeared to find a phone. "Courtney?" he called gently lifting her into his lap and cradling her with his arm, wincing when his shoulder twinged. Checking her pulse, he breathed easier feeling the strong beat beneath his fingers. "Courtney, can you hear me?"

He stroked her forehead moving the matted hair from her face and gently tapped her cheek.

"Courtney?" he called again.

She moaned and moved slightly. The maid ran back in with hotel security and the manager.

"Officer?" the manager asked.

"Lieutenant Greene," Jon provided. "This is Detective Shields, she's my partner."

His eyes drifted to the hotel maid who was looking through the closet and pulled out Courtney's raincoat. Walking over to him, she gently laid the coat over Courtney's front adding another layer for her modesty.

"The ambulance is on the way. Do you know what happened?" the manager asked.

"No," Jon replied. "But she's coming 'round, she'll know."

The maid stepped forward and spoke low. "I'm sorry, I don't know much English," Jon stopped her and spoke in Spanish. Her eyes lit and she smiled softly as she spoke to him in her language. "I'll make her a cup of tea with extra sugar. While I'm doing that, I have these," she pulled out a sweet treat and offered it to Jon. "It's basically sugar. It may help her."

"Thank you," Jon replied but shook his head. Understanding his concern, she nodded and left the room to make the tea.

Courtney moaned again and her forehead constricted.

"Courtney," he whispered. She moaned again but finally opened her eyes and looked unfocused on Jon.

"Hey," he smiled at her. "You're okay."

"Jon?" she groaned. "What happened?"

"What do you remember?" Jon asked.

"Oh, my head," she slowly lifted a hand to her head.

"Yeah, you'll be sore," he said.

"I was..." she tried to remember. "I was taking a bath and when I came out... I don't remember." She looked down at herself and saw she was wrapped in a hotel towel and her raincoat. "Great," she said.

"You're covered," he said. "Let's get you up. Can you sit up?"

She nodded and, with his help, she leaned against his chest. Scooting, she propped up against the foot of the bed and away from his bad shoulder. She held the towel tightly making sure it would not ride down over her chest.

"Let's get you dressed. I've sent for an ambulance," he said standing. Turning to see the manager still there, he raised his brows and the manager took a step back.

"I'll be just outside," he said. Jon waited until the door was shut then helped Courtney stand enough to sit on the edge of the bed.

Once she was settled, Jon picked up some of her clothes that had been ripped from the suitcase. Getting her needed items, even some she was too groggy to be embarrassed about, he set a pair of sweats, an oversized t-shirt and underwear on the bed. He turned away but was within reaching distance as she pulled on her clothes. Once she was dressed, he turned back to her and helped her lie propped up on the bed. Getting her comfortable, he pulled the sheets over her and went to the door. The manager, maid and several EMTs stood outside.

Jon walked with the emergency medical team and explained what he knew of the situation which was limited at best but at least he had felt the knot on the back of her head and gave them a starting point.

Jon turned to the General Manager and hotel security.

"I offer you our most sincerely apologies, Lieutenant," the GM started. "Nothing like this has ever happened in my hotel before."

"Thank you," Jon said. "But I would like to see the security footage of this floor for the past two hours. We are consulting with the MPD and I believe this has something to do with a case we are working on."

"Of course," the GM replied and gave the security team a nod. Jon's eyes kept drifting to Courtney as she sat with the EMTs. "Is there anything we can get you?"

"If there's anyone in the kitchens I think my partner should eat something," Jon said.

"I have tea here," the maid offered.

Jon thanked her but before he gave the cup to Courtney, he took a large gulp to make sure there was nothing wrong with it. Too sweet for him, he grimaced but when nothing happened, he thanked her and handed it to Courtney.

The maid tentatively went up to Jon and spoke softly in Spanish. "I know they make good food here, but I think she needs something a little sturdier. Does she like Mexican food?"

"I believe she would like that very much," Jon answered.

"And what is your favorite dish?" she asked as her cheeks flamed red with embarrassment.

"Am I obvious?" he asked gently.

"You know my language," she replied. "I would assume you

know my culture too."

"My wife was Spanish," Jon replied. "Born in El Paso."

"Then I know exactly what to make for you," she said and disappeared out of the room.

"I will have that footage on a disk for you, Lieutenant," the GM said. "Is there anything else?"

"That should be it," he answered.

"If you need me, my extension is 098," he said and left the room.

Jon turned back to where the EMTs worked on Courtney.

"Are you her husband?" one of the EMTs asked.

"Her partner," Jon replied showing his badge.

"She's agreed I tell you and has refused to go to the hospital," the EMT said. "She does not have a concussion and the swelling on the back of her head has gone down which is a good sign. Some ice, ibuprofen and rest is what she needs. When she does sleep, ask her questions when she wakes up. If she is unable to answer, take her to the hospital immediately."

"Understood," Jon said. "Can she eat something?"

"That would be best," she answered. "She should have something nutritious for the medicine to take effect."

Once the EMTs left the room, Jon went over to Courtney. Sitting on the bed, he took her hand.

"How are you feeling now?" he asked.

"I have a massive headache," she replied slurring her words a little. "But I'm better."

"Good," he said. "God, you scared the life out of me."

"I thought I saw some more grey hairs," she teased. He let out a strained laugh.

"What happened?" he asked after a beat.

"From what I can remember," she replied. "It all happened so quickly. I don't know what I saw."

"What do you think you saw?" he asked.

"Someone in here," she motioned to the wall to her left. "It's as if they were waiting for me."

"Did you hear anything?" he asked.

She shook her head. "Nothing, that's what's so weird."

"Okay," he pushed her hair away from her face. "You scared me, Courtney," he whispered. She had never heard him speak so softly.

"Hey," she said slipping her hand under his prickly chin. "I'm okay."

His green eyes were dark with stress as he took a deep breath and nodded.

"What do you think they were looking for?" she asked looking around the room.

"I have no idea," Jon replied. "Scare tactic?"

"But why?" she asked.

"Do they need a reason?" He asked. "Yet more proof we need to get back home."

She nodded in agreement but a knock at her door startled her. The hotel maid smiled up at Jon as he opened the door. The aroma of food on the tray she carried, tempting. He thanked her and opened the door wider for her to come in.

"I hope you like," she said to Courtney.

"I'm sure I will, thank you. And thank you for the tea, it made me feel better," Courtney said. The woman looked up at Jon confused. He translated and she smiled back at her.

Jon saw her to the door but she turned and spoke softly. "I made you some flan, I hope you enjoy."

"Oh, I haven't had good flan since my wife died," his tone was appreciative.

Her eyes softened and she cupped his face. "I saw sadness in your eyes. I am sorry for all you have lost."

"Thank you," he said. She nodded once and left the room.

"New girlfriend, Jon?" Courtney asked when he walked back.

"I like to keep my options open," he teased.

"I'll be sure to let Beth know," she replied accepting her plate from him.

"Ehm, I wish you wouldn't. I like my current sleeping arrangements," he replied.

They ate in silence except for the occasional moan of appreciation for the food. Once they were finished eating the best flan Jon had had since Carol died, Courtney yawned.

"I'm really tired," she said.

"They said you should rest. But I don't want you sleeping in here. Come to my room and lie down. I need to go and see what's taking so long on the security tapes. Will you be all right?"

"I'll be fine," she smiled. "I'm gonna lie down for a bit."

Jon helped her up and walked with her to his room. When she fell on to the bed, Jon went back to her room, grabbed her suitcase and the clothes on the floor. Packing up, he brought the duffle bag into his room and set it on the chair by the window. Courtney was asleep before he finished. Making sure he had everything, he locked her adjoining door and left through the main door. Going back into his room, he shut and locked the adjoining door on his side and set her gun on the nightstand. Kissing her hair as she slept, he whispered he would be right back. Slipping silently out of the room, he made his way to the elevator, pulling out his phone.

"Leave a message," the voicemail answered.

"Skylark," Jon said. "I repeat Skylark. Hotel, twenty minutes ago." He hung up and pushed the elevator button.

Chapter
Thirty-Two

Viktor walked into the village pub. After looking all over the castle, grounds, stables, and forest for Iollan, the village was the last place he could think of. It had been nearly seven hours since anyone had seen him. Knowing Iollan shouldn't be alone after hearing about his parent's divorce, Viktor finally found him sitting at the bar, a glass of whiskey dangling between his middle finger and thumb. Walking over, he slid onto the stool beside him. McGriffit, the pubkeeper, locked eyes with Viktor while he dried a glass and shook his head. Iollan was further gone than he thought.

"Pint, please, Griff," Viktor ordered cheerfully. McGriffit nodded and began pouring a Guinness.

"Whatda you want?" Iollan's voice was slurred.

"A drink," he dug out four two euro coins and handed it to McGriffit as he handed him his beer. The drinking age in Ireland was lower than America and having just turned nineteen a month ago, Viktor developed a taste for Guinness.

"Did me da' send ye out to check on me?" Iollan asked.

Viktor had a slight difficulty understanding Iollan's accent when he was sober, but when he was drunk, his accent was more pronounced. However, Viktor did understand some words and was able to infer the rest.

"No," Viktor said. "I was worried about you and figured, when I saw Lucky in the stable, you must be here. I didn't know if you wanted to talk."

"Oh, aye?" Iollan asked. "Tat's what's bloody wrong with you damn Americans... ye're all talky-feely... We Irishmen donnat *have* ta talk about everythin' on our min's."

"Maybe that's why you guys drink so much," Viktor shrugged taking a swig of his beer chuckling to himself at how Iollan didn't finish a word.

"Hey!" Iollan yelled. Then lowered his voice to him. "Don't talk ta me."

"That's going to be difficult," Viktor said calmly.

"I donnat undastand ya," Iollan replied his speech slurring even more. "Why are you even here? It's no' like you belong... Oy! McGriffit! What am I paying ya fer? Fill 'er up!"

McGriffit sighed under his breath and looked over at Viktor. Pulling out the bottle, he poured a single in Iollan's glass but Iollan grabbed the bottle from the pubkeeper and poured more. McGriffit took it back from him and hid it underneath the bar.

"I mean serisly," Iollan went on taking a gulp. "You aren't Irish, like."

"No, but I'd like to be," Viktor said.

"And you're *no'* me brother... I doonat care what *he* says. You willnit take me place as his son, ya hear?" Iollan replied.

"Is that what this is all about?" Viktor asked. "Iollan, I swear to you I would *never* want to take your place. I could never run this whole place. I wasn't trained since birth. I'm not blood. It's your place and not mine. I swear to you."

"Why no'?" Iollan yelled. "Me life's already fallin' down around me... why no'? Tat's just what I need!" Iollan toasted the air and tossed back the whiskey. As he did, he tilted back a little too far and fell backwards off the stool. Viktor hopped off and helped him up.

"Damn," Iollan cursed. "Bloody waste of good whiskey..." he pulled his shirt up and tried to lick the whiskey off the fabric where it spilled.

"I don't think you can handle anymore," Viktor said hooking his arms around his shoulders. "Let's go home."

"Sorry, but I donnat go tat way," Iollan slurred and started giggling.

"Come on," Viktor got him up and handed McGriffit the whiskey glass. Pulling out his wallet while trying to keep Iollan upright. McGriffit held up his hand.

"Just get him home, aye?" he said.

"Cheers," Viktor replied and started them towards the door.

"Where'd we going?" Iollan demanded in his drunken slur. "Where's me drink? McGriffit?"

"I think you've had plenty," Viktor said trying to keep him upright and walking towards the door.

"Donnat tell me what ta do!" Iollan replied. "You're no' me da'."

"No, I'm not," Viktor agreed. "I'm your friend and I want to take care of you."

"Are we?" Iollan asked. "Are we friends? I donnat even know your real name. What kinda friend does tat?"

Viktor was quiet for a moment.

"It's Viktor," he finally admitted.

"Vik-" Iollan hiccupped. "Tor? Tat doesn't suit you. Ooh, shiny!"

Iollan broke away from him and stumbled towards a window of one of the shops.

"No, no, we're going home," Viktor said pulling Iollan back.

"Where's me drink?" He demanded. "McGriffit! Bring me another whiskey!"

"You've had enough," Viktor replied.

Iollan pulled away from him and ran to a patch of grass beside the shop. Gripping the brick corner, he vomited into the foliage. Viktor went over to help him up.

"Just leave me alone!" Iollan shouted pushing him away with his free hand.

"I can't do that," Viktor said.

"Why? 'Cause yer me *friend?*" Iollan sneered.

"Yeah, pretty much," Viktor said reaching for Iollan's arm. "Come on."

"No, no," Iollan replied pulling away from him and stumbling. "No, stop it!"

Iollan swung at him, his fist colliding with Viktor's cheek causing both to stumble back. Iollan landed hard on his rear. Viktor prodded the area where Iollan's drunken punch had collided with his cheekbone. It wasn't too bad but it ached horribly. Bending his knees up and resting his arms over them, Iollan hung his head and cried. Viktor walked back to him, bent down to be eye level and placed a hand on his friend's arm. Iollan looked up at him, sniffling.

"Come on, man, let me get you home," Viktor said quietly.

"I'm sorry," Iollan replied.

"Eh, don't worry about it. It's nothing I can't handle," Viktor answered.

"I'm completely bolloxed."

"I don't know what that means but okay," Viktor grinned. "Let me help you. I'll get you home."

Viktor grabbed his friend under his arm and helped pull him to his feet. Iollan weaved for a moment but Viktor put his arm around his waist and wrapped Iollan's arm around his shoulders. They walked together slowly and silently for a time. Once the castle was in sight, Iollan broke the silence.

"Greg?" he said.

"Yeah, man?" Viktor asked.

"Are you gay?" he asked. Viktor's step faltered but, before they both crashed headfirst into the gravel, he righted and cleared his throat.

"Uhm," Viktor said. "Why do you ask?"

"I've never seen you with a woman," he replied. "Like ever."

"I'm... not sure," he admitted.

"What'dya mean? It's either you like women or you like men," Iollan said. "What's there to be confused about?"

"A lot," he answered. "But sex... isn't something on my radar at the moment."

"Well whenever it is..." Iollan patted his shoulder a little too hard. "You lemme know. I know some women who will help you make up your mind." He giggled then and didn't stop until he landed on his bed passed out drunk.

Chapter
Thirty-Three

Jon returned to his room about half an hour later. Quietly opening the door, he stuck his head in when he heard Courtney talking. She was sitting up in bed talking on the phone. She saw him and mouthed, Ryan. He nodded and went to the TV. Courtney finally hung up the phone and looked at Jon's back as he fiddled with the DVD player.

"I couldn't sleep for more than twenty minutes so I wanted to call my mom and Ryan," she said.

"Good, I'm sure your mom isn't happy with me," he said.

"She's not happy with the situation," she replied. "But she wouldn't blame you."

"How are you feeling?" Jon asked turning back and walking over to the bed, sitting on the edge.

"My head still hurts," she replied. "Ryan gave me a great

suggestion that I might need your help with."

"Anything," he said.

"Ice for twenty minutes, off for twenty then ice again," she replied. "He said it would help with the swelling."

"I'll pop out to the drugstore around the corner and get an icepack," Jon said. "I have some ice already but it'll be easier with a pack. I'll get that for you then I wanna watch this."

"Thanks," she smiled. He stood, but she grasped his hand and looked up at him. "With everything that's happened, I haven't asked how you're doing." Her hand ghosted over his shoulder.

"I'm fine," he replied. "Yes, it's a little stiff and yeah, I get twinges of pain now and again but on the whole, I'll be fine, as will you."

"I know," she answered.

"You've been through hell, it's okay to let it out," he swiped a hand over the top of her head to push back some hair.

"This isn't the first time I've experienced this sort of thing, Jon," she answered. "I'm fine. If I'm not, I will let you know."

"Good, but you know you don't have to be so tough around me."

"Likewise," she replied.

"Touché," he answered. "I'll get you that ice." He scoped out ice into a bag, tied it off and wrapped it in one of his t-shirts then quickly left the room and headed to his car. After finding the pharmacy around the corner, he purchased two icepacks, a couple candy bars and a tub of Courtney's favorite ice cream. Courtney was flipping through the channels but sat up with he arrived.

"I got some goodies too," he set out the sweets he purchased.

"Ooh, how did you know? I almost texted you."

"Been married, remember? I know women's cravings," he teased.

"Shut up," she laughed. "I'm not pregnant nor is it that time of the month."

"No, that's not what I meant," he replied. "I just meant I thought you might like it."

"Love it," she answered watching as he went to the small bar area to put the ice packs into the freezer and popped the dry ice one, shook it and handed it to her.

"I want to see the security tapes, did you get them?" she asked accepting the ice and the treats.

"I've got the copy right here," he queued up the player.

The grainy picture of a security camera came on the screen and Jon sat on the foot of the bed as they watched.

Fast forwarding to when they saw themselves arrive back at the hotel, Jon grabbed two water bottles from the mini fridge and took a seat beside her, his back resting against the headboard.

"You know what this reminds me of?" Jon asked. Courtney lazily looked over at him and shook her head. "A month ago, the first time you met Steven when we were looking through security footage from Pastor Holywell's security system."

"Oh yeah, though I fell asleep," she smiled.

"And stole my coffee," he winked.

"That's not how I remember it," she replied.

"Oh no?" Jon chuckled, then after a moment he sobered and took a deep breath. "What a broken pair we are."

"No, not broken," she stated. "Definitely not broken. Seasoned, experienced, matured, definitely but not broken."

He took her hand and threaded their fingers together. Raising them to his lips, he kissed her knuckles and smiled softly. "No, not broken," he agreed. Without another word, they turned back to the screen and kept watch.

A moment later the elevator doors opened and a businessman in a black suit walked out, rolling his weekend suitcase behind him. He walked down the hallway to his room. Not five minutes later, the elevator doors opened again and a blonde woman along with Brent Tyler walked out. Jon's whole body tensed.

"Is that her? Is that Scott's ex-wife?" Courtney asked.

"Older, but yeah, that's Meredith," Jon said.

"She's... stunning," she replied.

"Gorgeous, on the outside only," Jon answered. "But at nineteen, I'm afraid my son wasn't concerned with inner beauty."

"What nineteen year old would be?" she asked.

They watched as Brent waited outside Courtney's room and Meredith went inside. A cold chill ran down Courtney's back. She watched Jon's jaw flex and his hand gripped the remote tightly.

Before Meredith left the room, Brent pulled out his phone and started typing something.

"Can you get closer and see what he's typing?" Courtney asked.

"Wouldn't do much," Jon replied. "It's blurry already."

Just then, Jon's phone rang and the name Skylark appeared on the screen.

Answering it, with a simple "yeah" he put it on speaker.

"It's me," Steven said. "We got your message. Brent told me what happened. Is she all right?"

"She's fine," Jon answered. "No concussion."

"Good," Steven replied. "Listen I got a text from Brent earlier and when we got your message, I knew I needed to call you."

"What did he say?" Jon asked.

"Well, it's a love poem," Steven's voice held a chuckle. "'Remember when we saw each other that night? The music, the drinks, the dancing? I'll never forget how the midnight sky lit up with your presence. I'll be lonely tonight thinking of you...' Brent's not one for poetry."

"Got it," Jon replied.

"Gotta go," Steven answered and abruptly hung up.

"So," Jon said turning to Courtney.

"Outside that Irish restaurant tonight, midnight," she said unscrambling Brent's message.

"Do you feel up to it?" Jon asked.

"I think so," she said. "But right now, I really want some ice cream." Jon chuckled and reached for it.

———◦◦———

Viktor finally got Iollan back to the castle. Heading up the narrow backstairs, Viktor worried, more than once, Iollan would slip and take him down too but the backstairs was away from the rest of the house and hardly used anymore. If Iollan was as loud as he was at the pub, Viktor didn't want him waking the entire household. Luckily, Iollan quieted down and Viktor got him to his room. His cheek was aching from Iollan's drunken punch. Opening the door to Iollan's room, Viktor got him to the bed. Without so much as taking off his shoes, Iollan fell into bed, nearly taking Viktor down with him. Steading and straightening, Viktor pulled off Iollan's boots and covered him with the blanket. Iollan mumbled something in his sleep and sunk deeper into the pillow.

After making sure he was all right, Viktor quietly left his room, shutting the door behind him.

"Greg?" a soft voice in the darkness startled him. Kathleen stood in her bedroom doorway and Viktor could see the orange glow of her fireplace behind her. "Is everything all right, love?"

"Yeah, he's just a little drunk," Viktor said.

Kathleen nodded slightly and took a step towards him. She reached for his cheek seeing the fresh bruise and a little dried blood.

"What happened?" she asked.

"I... uh... walked into a door," he covered.

"You're a good friend to him," she said.

"He was drunk," Viktor justified.

"Come with me," she said. "Let's get that cleaned up."

He smiled slightly at the woman who had become like a grandmother to him. "I've had worse," he said walking into her room.

"I know," she answered. "But that's on the same cheek as your fracture."

Viktor sighed. He had forgotten about that. That's why it hurt a lot more than usual.

"Let me take care of you," she smiled as she disappeared into her *ensuite* bathroom. He sat beside the fireplace and closed his eyes for a moment.

"It's really nothing," he said, although his head ached something fierce.

"I'm a mother, sweetheart," she called. "You're not going to be able to stop me," she smiled softly at him as she left the bathroom with a few items in her hand.

"I guess I'm not used to people taking care of me," he said.

She poured a little alcohol on a cotton ball and dotted his cheek. He flinched at the sting.

"Oh, sorry," she said. After cleaning the slight cut, she put a bandage on it.

"Thank you," he smiled. Leaning forward, she kissed Band-Aid.

"That's the most important part," she smiled.

"You seem to be a pro at this."

"Oh, my son got into some fights," she said.

"Really?" He looked at her surprised. "I can't see Jon getting into any fights."

"Oh, not many, his biggest fight was with Keelan," she went on.

"What? What happened?" Viktor asked.

"Jon and Siobhan, that's Keelan's sister, dated for a while. She found out that he was also seeing Beth back in America. She was not as upset as her brother. See, both she and Jon were seeing other people when they weren't together. But Keelan was angry saying, when you're with someone you should be with them mind, body and soul until you die, so they had a big fight."

"I can't see Jon doing that," Viktor said.

"He was your age once," she teased. "He was a flirt."

"But for Keelan too? I guess this whole thing with his divorce is terrible for him," Viktor replied.

"I can imagine what he's going through and I wouldn't wish it on anyone," she said. "But I hope he doesn't let this ruin him. He has so much to live for and so many people who love him."

"Can I ask you something?" he asked.

"Of course," she answered.

"I saw something between Keelan and Maighdhlin earlier today," he began. "Is there something going on there?"

Kathleen sighed. "I can't say without breaking a confidence," she replied. "But I will tell you, he has never acted on his feelings for Maighdhlin. He has been nothing but a complete gentleman."

"I expected no less," Viktor said. "I just hope he doesn't wait too long."

"You and me both, son," she agreed. Viktor yawned and flinched as his cheek throbbed.

"He probably won't remember," he said indicating the bruise. "Please, if anyone asks…"

"You ran into the stable door," she confirmed.

"Thanks," he said standing.

"Greg," she called him back and he looked back at her. "You are such a blessing to all of us here. I want you to know that."

"Thank you," he said as a small lump formed in his throat. He swallowed it away, smiled slightly and headed to his room.

Chapter
Thirty-Four

*V*iktor *heard his cell phone ring on the night stand. He woke,*
took it without looking at the number and answered.

"Hello?" he said. There was no answer. "Hello? Is someone
there?" This time there was someone breathing on the other end. "Hello?"
he said again, this time with more urgency.

"Did you think you could escape me?" a voice he would never,
could never forget said on the other end. His father had found him. He
swallowed hard.

"F–father?" he stuttered.

"How's Ireland, Vitya?" his father asked. "Come downstairs, I
have present for you."

Immediately, Viktor hung up the phone, tore the sheets off him
and raced to the door. He heard someone scream in the entryway and
rushed to the top of the stairs to look over the balustrade. His father stood

with a group of his men behind him. Keelan, Iollan, Kathleen, several of the servants and Sergei were on their knees with their hands behind their heads. A line of his father's men stood behind them, each of his friends had guns aimed at the back of their heads.

"It's good to see you, Viktor," his father looked up at him. "It's been a long time. You know what you put me through? Why would you want to do that?"

Viktor swallowed and tried to breathe but no matter how much his lungs burned with the need for air, he couldn't draw a breath. He stood frozen at the top of the stairs.

"You've hurt me, Viktor," his father continued.

"Father, please," he finally got out.

His father sighed, turned slightly and nodded to his men. Viktor watched in horror as all the people he loved were shot in the head and fell forward dead.

"No!" He screamed.

"Wake up, Greg. You're safe," Keelan called. "Vitya, wake up."

Viktor's eyes flew open as he gasped for air. His body was covered in a cold sweat and the sheets were tangled around his knees. Looking over, his eyes finally adjusting, he saw Keelan sitting on his bed, alive.

"You were having a nightmare," Keelan said. Viktor locked eyes with him and, in a quick movement, sat up and threw his arms around Keelan. Surprised at first, Keelan tentatively hugged him back. "It's all right." He soothed Viktor's hair. "You're safe. Everything is all right."

"I'm sorry," Viktor fought against the lump in his throat.

"It's all right, lad," Keelan replied.

Finally, Viktor pulled back and looked up at Keelan. Only then did Keelan see the bandage and bruise on his face.

"What happened?" Keelan asked.

"It's nothing."

"Vitya?" Keelan pressed.

"I... walked into a door."

"Did Iollan do that?" he asked. Viktor's eyes widened and Keelan sighed. "He should never have taken it out on you. What was he thinking?"

"No, he didn't mean to," Viktor defended. "He was... drunk."

"I'm sorry you took the brunt of my son's anger," he huffed. "I'll have a talk with him."

"He didn't mean to do it," Viktor said again.

"Where is he now?" Keelan asked.

"I got him to his room, he passed out," he explained.

Keelan nodded thanking him but changed the subject. "You want to talk about your night terror?" Keelan asked.

"Not really," he answered. "But I will if it'll help you."

"It would. Let's go down to the library," Keelan said. "I'll lay a fire. Pour us some whiskey?"

Viktor nodded and got out of bed pulling on a shirt.

———◦◦———

Jon and Courtney pulled up to the designated meeting place. They waited until a quarter past midnight but there was no one there. Frowning, Jon pulled out his phone and read the text Steven had forwarded to him. He reread it out loud to make sure they hadn't misread it.

Remember when we saw each other that night? The music, the drinks, the dancing? I'll never forget how the midnight sky lit up with your presence. I'll be lonely tonight thinking of you...

"Well," Courtney started, her head pounding from the attack that day. "There's no one here." She tried for civil, she didn't want Jon to know she wasn't feeling up to it. It came out snippier than she had intended, and Jon raised an eyebrow.

"Let's wait another fifteen minutes," Jon said.

Leaning her head back, she closed her eyes for a moment. What felt like a second later, Jon tapped her knee, waking her. The clock showed she had been asleep for twenty minutes.

"Look," Jon whispered, seeing a white van pull up under the only other streetlamp. They both watched as the brake lights flashed twice. "Let's go." Jon said reaching for the door and getting out. The brake lights started flashing erratically.

"Get back to the car," Jon hissed. "I have a bad feeling about this." But just as they started walking back to Jon's car, the back of the van opened and Adam Pellegrino appeared with a machine gun opening fire on them. They ducked into Jon's Escalade and thanked their lucky stars for the bullet proof glass Jon had fitted after the explosion at the hospital two months ago. As soon as the doors were shut Jon threw the car into reverse and slammed down the pedal. Skidding on the wet pavement, the car lurched back and drew them away from the gunfire.

"Thank god for bullet proof glass," Courtney said as soon as they were well enough away.

"A little extra expense I thought was needed," Jon replied.

"I agree, just keep driving," Courtney said holding onto the hand hold as Jon took a corner a little too fast.

They were quiet for a long time until Jon broke the silence. "You know we can't go back to the hotel, right?"

"Yeah…" she answered. "Where do we go?"

"Somewhere not in Minneapolis," he replied. "We'll head southeast toward Indy, find a place to lay low and I'll go back and get our things."

"What do you think they did to Brent?" she finally asked.

Jon's hands gripped the steering wheel tighter, but he didn't answer. He didn't need to, she already knew.

"Is there anything hidden in your room you'll need me to get?" Jon asked.

She shook her head looking down at her ring.

"Just be sure to get the picture of Ryan and me on the night stand," she pleaded.

"I will," he replied. "Promise."

Chapter
Thirty-Five

After driving for thirty minutes, Jon pulled off at the first sign of an Holiday Inn Express. Checking in, he and Courtney went up to their room. He had opted for one room with two queens instead of separate rooms. After she was settled, Jon promised to be quick and keep in contact with her, then left the hotel. As he drove back to Minneapolis, he called Dave.

"Are you all right?" Dave answered. Well past midnight in Indianapolis, Dave's voice sounded rough as if he had yet to get to sleep.

"No," Jon replied. "And I doubt the guy helping us is still alive."

Dave was silent on the other end for a long moment. "What... uh... what do you mean?"

"There was a man helping us, he works with Steven, his

name is Brent Tyler, I'm fairly certain he was found out."

Again, Dave was quiet, then clearing his throat, he continued. "We'll... um... contact his family."

"I'd like to know if I can do that," Jon said. "The man is an American Patriot."

"I'm sure that would be fine," Dave's voice was broken as he spoke but soon he cleared his throat again and continued. "What happened? Where's Shields?"

"She was attacked, I drove her to a hotel and am going back to Minneapolis to get our things."

"Is she all right?"

"Yes," Jon sighed. "But it's time for us to leave. Let the big guns handle this. It's a shit show."

"That's what I've been trying to tell you," Dave replied.

"I know," Jon answered. "But it's our job."

"Have you talked to Steven? Where is he?"

"Silent," Jon said. "Last I heard, he sent us a text from Brent."

"Come home, we'll contact him together."

"Good idea," Jon answered. "Besides there are more agents in the field and I'm not going to be responsible for another agent's death."

"Get home and be safe."

"Already pulling into the outskirts of Minneapolis. As soon as I get our things, I'll be back with Courtney and we will be home tomorrow evening."

"Be careful, Jon," Dave cautioned. "Let me know when you leave for home."

"Will do," Jon promised. "If you talk to Steven, please ask him about Brent. He was a great kid."

"I will," Dave swore but his voice was tight again. Jon hung up and pulled into the parking garage attached to the hotel.

———————

The last town passed the window in a snowy blur as Zoe looked out the car's window. Having gone radio silent to keep her cover, she had no hope of backup and the further Eammon O'Malley drove the more she was inclined to believe it was a suicide mission.

"Where are we going, E?" she asked hoping her voice was light enough he wouldn't think anything of it.

"A friend of mine has a place up here, darlin'," he replied. "I thought a little alone time would be good."

"But don't you have work?" she asked.

"Aye, but I can do that from anywhere," he answered. "Although I should probably warn you, we'll have some company tonight. I'm trying to close a deal and they've been slippery."

"But we'll be alone after that, right?"

"As alone as we can be with my security," he chuckled.

"That's all I want," she replied sliding her hand over his thick thigh and slipping it higher trying to distract him. He side-glanced at her but stopped her hand with his and slid it back down to his knee, giving it two pats for good measure.

"Later, darlin'," he promised. She had long ago mastered her body's inherent responses and the shiver of disgust that snaked down her spine was well hidden behind her Mata Hari smile.

"So long as you promise," she said.

"Trust me, there's a lot we need to talk about, we'll be alone," he replied.

And just like that the butterflies fluttered again. Gazing out the window, she closed her eyes for a brief moment hoping to quell the sickening feeling that this road led to her death.

Chapter Thirty-Six

Radio Silence meant going dark and, as many times as Steven had done it as an agent, he hated it as a handler.

When his phone rang, he jumped and checked the ID. Sighing when he saw the name, he clicked answer.

"He called you, didn't he?" Steven asked.

"Yes," the man answered. "Tell me what happened."

"Radio Silence," Steven replied.

"Is he alive?" The tension in the man's voice gutted Steven.

"I don't know," Steven answered. "Last I heard, he was, but..."

"Could he have had to change the plan?"

"I hope not, he would have had to give them something and it might have been Zoe."

"He wouldn't do that," the man argued.

"I don't want to think he would, but this whole damn thing with Jon messed up a perfectly laid plan."

"I know," he sighed. "He's on his way back but I fear the damage may already be done. Do you have a way to contact Zoe?"

"She has a Sat. phone, but other than that, no. O'Malley is taking her up to a cabin in the mountains of Canada."

"He's crossed the border?" The man asked.

"That doesn't matter much," Steven replied.

"Tell me as soon as you hear anything," the man ordered.

"I will. I'm sure Brent will be all right."

"He better be," he stated then hung up.

Zoe stepped over the threshold and shrugged out of her heavy winter coat. Eammon walked in behind her and, true to her character of Katie, she turned to him, a blinding smile on her face as she squealed.

Racing into his open arms, she threw hers around his neck and kissed him hard. His tight grip and rocking of his slightly overweight body against her made her mind rebel against what was happening.

"Do you have to have that meeting tonight?" she whispered huskily in his ear. He chuckled but pushed her slightly away from him. Never a good sign.

"It's a deal I have to make," he said.

"Are you sure there isn't *any* way I can convince you?" she rubbed against him, hoping to distract him enough.

"Ah, *cailin*," he sighed and stepped away from her. "I wish I had the time. But go, up the stairs and through the second door on the right is the master bath. Relax, have a glass of wine. I'll be up to get you when they leave."

"Promise?" she asked.

"I do," he swore. "Now go."

She slowly walked away from him determined to make him want her and distract him from what she thought might be happening. She climbed the stair and shed piece after piece of her clothes knowing his eyes were on her.

As soon as the door was shut, she hurried to the window and raised the glass. Bars greeted her as well as the long expanse of Riding Mountain National Park. The sun set quickly there and as the last rays of day slipped behind the massive range before her, a shiver raced up her spine. Unable to check in with Steven after Brent disappeared, she hated the part of her that believed she had been burned.

Hearing the front door open and Eammon greet whoever it was, she threw on a sweater and jeans, eased the bedroom door open and looked over the banister. Eammon O'Malley greet Adam Pellegrino and Viktor Redorvsky Senior. Her heart sped up. If those three were under the same roof, it could only mean one thing, the *deal* O'Malley had to make was exactly what Steven's intel had said.

Redorvsky specialized in money laundering and racketeering. O'Malley in sex trafficking and Pellegrino, a dirty police chief, came from a long line of arms dealers and kept the police at bay.

There was no sign of Brent but the way Meredith sauntered in and slipped her arm through Pellegrino's showed she pretty much ran the show. The other two men greeted her with a kiss. Pulling out her phone, Zoe knew there was no service but if she could record the meeting and upload it, she prayed it would go through when/if she got service.

As noiselessly as she could, she began recording the meeting.

Chapter Thirty-Seven

"And over there is the library, it houses the Book of Kells, a beautiful early century manuscript," Iollan explained as he and Viktor walked around the grounds of Trinity College in Dublin. Viktor nodded but didn't answer, his mind elsewhere. Iollan didn't speak for a little while, but as soon as they came upon a park bench, he sat down in a huff. "Do you want me to drive us back home?"

"What?" Viktor looked over at him. "No, why?"

"You're no' paying any attention and I know why," he sighed and leaned forward, resting his elbows on his knees. "I'm so sorry I hit you," he started. "I would say it was because I was drunk, but that's no excuse."

"Iollan, what are you talking about?" Viktor asked.

"I can see the bruise," he indicated Viktor's cheek. "I know it was when I smashed but I'm so sorry."

"It's not your fault," Viktor rushed to say and sat beside his friend. "We were both going through a lot. I'm sorry you have to go through this. We all handle stress differently."

"It's no excuse for hitting my friend when you're just trying to help," he replied. "I thought it was a dream then, when I saw your cheek the way it is, I knew it wasn't. I'm sorry. With the wedding being planned, I never thought to be that person. Split parents at my wedding, like."

"I know," Viktor said. "I've never thought about getting married, but I can't imagine how that would be."

"Why don't you ever think about being married?"

"Not interested, I guess."

"In marriage or in women?" Iollan asked gently.

"You asked me that already," Viktor sighed. "What is it you want to know? Am I interested in men? No. Am I interested in women? Not really."

"Have you ever?"

"With a man like my father, there wasn't any time to be the rebellious teenager and sleep around. I just don't know. There was someone... once. He works for my father. He and I... it's complicated. He's married, or at least he was. Before I left, he told me he was getting a divorce."

"It's none of my business. I'm sorry. I just wanted to know more about you. But I understand what it's like," Iollan said.

"You do?" Viktor laughed not meaning to sound skeptical but couldn't help it.

"Not in the way you think, but being the heir to the estate's stewardship and having four older brothers who were like fathers and yet constantly arguing with each other, it prevented having outside friends. But at least I had Scott for a little while and again now. You have no one. I can only imagine what that was like for you."

"Sergei was... is my friend," Viktor said and looked down. "My one and only friend. But things got... complicated when feelings were explored."

"Feelings will do that. Complicate things. I'm grateful you told me," he said. "Just know you have me as a friend, brother, or just an ear. I care about you. If you need someone to talk to just know, nothing you say could ever hurt our friendship unless you threaten my family or the Greenes but I doubt you would do that."

"Never, and thank you," Viktor said.

"Could I ask you something else?" Viktor nodded but said nothing. "Would you be one of my groomsmen?"

Viktor blinked in surprise but a slow smile lifted the corners of his mouth.

"I would love to," he said.

"Grand," Iollan grinned.

"No one's ever asked me to be one. The only wedding I've been to was my friend's."

"Ahh, the *complicated* one?" Iollan asked. Viktor blanched but nodded. "Well," Iollan slapped his back. "It's not too difficult, just make sure my best man doesn't get drunk."

"Who's going to be your best man?"

"Scott," Iollan replied. "At least I hope so, I haven't asked him yet."

"That'll be fun," Viktor said. "I am looking forward to meeting him again."

"He's a great guy. He'll be a great landlord," Iollan replied. "Anyway, I'm sorry I hit you. If you want me to drive you back I will."

"No, I don't want you to," Viktor answered. "I think we both need a break from what's going on at home."

"I want to help da' but he's shut me out," Iollan said after a brief pause.

"He's going through a lot too," Viktor replied. "Everything he's worked for during his life is crumbling. He's trying to find his footing. We all are."

"I'm so angry with ma," he said. "How could she do this?"

"Your mother lost two children," Viktor reminded him.

"And da' lost two sons, how does it make it all right?"

"It doesn't," Viktor said. "But how Keelan is handling things in his own way, your mother is handling things in hers. You have to handle them in yours."

Iollan huffed a sigh. "How did you get so wise?"

"A hard life," Viktor replied. "But I understand people. I can read them. I've heard I get that from my mother." Viktor looked away and off toward the bell tower.

"Any news on your da's case?" Iollan asked gently.

"No," Viktor sighed. "I just wish Jon would let me turn evidence over,"

"Look, I don't know much about your past and I sure as hell don't know what's going on, but one thing I do know for certainty is his lordship would never put you in harm's way. Trust him. He knows what he's doing."

"I've seen so much of my father's destruction I want him behind bars."

"Not at the risk of your life or anyone around you," Iollan said.

"It would be worth my life but not Jon's. I'd never want him hurt because of me."

"Then let him do what he feels is important," Iollan advised.

"I just feel helpless," he said.

Iollan laughed humorlessly, "join the club," he said. "But," he sighed, rubbed his hands on his jean clad thighs and stood. "Let's not worry about this now, hmm? How about we go to Temple Bar for a couple pints? My treat." he winked.

"Won't say no," Viktor said. "So long as food is involved."

"Expensive date," Iollan laughed. "Fine, I'll get you a Shephard's Pie. That do you?"

"Sounds good to me."

"First, I want to thank you all for coming on short notice," Zoe recognized Eammon's voice from behind the door. Creeping down the back staircase to follow them into Eammon's study, she kept her phone recording and uploading to the cloud if and when she got a signal. The cork on a bottle was popped softly as if wine or whiskey was being poured. The door was shut but the voices carried. "We all know each other so we can get started."

"What are we in the Godfather? Get on with it," what sounded like Pellegrino's voice came next.

"It's strange to me to be here with Italy and Ireland," Redorvsky's heavily accented voice came next. "We are making history with our three families. I want to take moment to express my gratitude to you, Pellegrino. Though your motives were self-serving, they helped me out of tight spot I found myself in."

"Because of your son," Pellegrino said. There was a pause. "Oh, don't give me that, closed casket? Family only? Did you even see the body? How do you know he's dead?"

"Sergei would not lie to me," Redorvsky replied.

"Any man can lie if given the right motivation and I heard he and your son were pretty close," Pellegrino continued. "I happen to have it on good authority that your son is still alive and living his days in Ireland at the expense of one Jonathan Greene, Lieutenant of the Indianapolis Police Department."

"You lie," Redorvsky spat.

"Gentlemen," Meredith calmed the situation. "We did not come here to make a scene. I understand it's difficult but we have a mutual enemy. Greene and Shields. Eammon, he left the IRA and you lost thousands of dollars on the deal you made. Viktor, he went after your son and flipped him, if the rumors are to be believed. You lost not only family, money but time, time you spent in prison waiting for us to plan a way around your arrest. And Adam, he's a thorn in your side since he first arrived. You've had to watch everything you say and do since he's been here. I say the time for games is over, it's time to act. He is in our way."

"It's not just him," Adam replied. "We have the CIA, NSA and Homeland on our tail. That bastard tried to warn Greene last night."

"You took care of him?" Redorvsky asked.

"I handled it, he's an asset now," Adam said. "What Meredith and I are proposing is a partnership further than Greene. Blend our families. Make it a nationwide, hell worldwide operation. My father is behind us and he has several other senators on his payroll. He even is flirting with the idea of a Presidential run. He has asked me to make you an offer. My sister is twenty-eight and by all accounts, beautiful. She knows her place in our family and would be agreeable to a marriage to strengthen our bond. Eammon, your boy Liam is thirty correct?"

"Aye," the Irishman replied.

"Would you be agreeable to a marriage between them should one be offered?"

There was silence for a long moment, then Eammon replied, "I believe that could be arranged. But I want the terms written up by a third party not one of your father's solicitors. I want one we can both agree on without ties to either. Redorvsky do you have any you would recommend?"

"A couple," he replied.

"Then I would consider it."

"When he handed the reigns of our family business over to me, he swore he'd always have my back. I'm planning on traveling to D.C. to meet with him later this month. If I can tell him we have come to an agreement, he will be pleased to do business with and for you at a discounted price of course."

"Tell me what you would ask in return," Redorvsky stated.

"I ask for nothing but loyalty. A loyalty between brothers and comrades. For too long we've been simple minded, walking around and running our businesses with blinders on. Don't you see? The true power comes from unity not diversity. The days of gentlemen mafia is over. However before we do that we need to get rid of Jonathan Greene."

"For one man, he seems to hold a lot of power," Eammon said.

"You swore to find him, didn't you?" Adam asked. "When he left you high and dry you swore vengeance. And Viktor when you were on the steps of the courthouse didn't you swear vengeance as well? It's time we start putting our money where our mouths are and do something about a man who has plagued us for too long."

Everyone was silent for a long time then a tinkling laugh sounded. "Oh gentlemen," Meredith said. "Do you honestly believe you are invincible alone? Eammon, you are still enjoying that little redheaded piece?" When no one replied, she went on. "Why don't you ask her what Skylark means?"

Zoe's heart stuttered to a stop for a moment then went into overdrive. Backing up, she tripped over a broom and fell, her phone skidding across the tile floor. Getting up, she didn't pay attention to the shouts coming from behind her, she ran. Just as she reached the front door, she cried out as someone grabbed her by the hair and yanked. She fell back and reached up to ease the pain. Looking over she saw one of Eammon O'Malley's body guards dragging her back. Eammon, Adam, Viktor, and Meredith all stood in the massive living room. Knowing if she didn't get out of there, they would kill her, she twisted and kicked the body guard but his hold was firm and painful.

As soon as they reached the four, the body guard threw her down in front of them.

"What is going on, Eammon?" She went for the dumb act.

"Don't give him that, little girl," Meredith said. "What are you, straight off the farm?"

"What?" She shook her head. "All I know is, I was looking for you and wanted some fresh air. It started snowing and I wanted to see it. Then I'm being dragged back here by my hair. What's going on, baby?"

Eammon was as stoic as stone as he glared down at her.

"Tell us now, what are you? FBI, NSA, CIA?" Redorvsky demanded.

"FBI? What? What are you talking about? Eammon?" She looked desperately over at him. "What's going on? Who are these people?"

"You can drop the act, sunshine," Adam said. "I'm sure if we press Brent a little more he'll give you up."

So, Tyler hadn't given her up. She felt a brief moment of gratitude followed by sorrow for her partner.

"Who is Brent?" she asked. "Eammon, you know me, baby, what's going on?"

"You know me, baby," Meredith mocked. "Ask her, Eammon. Ask her what Skylark means."

"Skylark?" She questioned. "What is she talking about?"

"Katie," Eammon finally spoke but his tone was hard. "If that is indeed your name. I will give you one chance. Answer me truthfully and I will consider what to do. What is Skylark?"

"Eammon, I have no idea," she pleaded.

He stared at her for a moment, then sighed. "Give me your phone, *Cailin.*"

"What?" She squeaked.

"Your phone, now," he ordered. When she hesitated, he scoffed and closed his eyes. "Oh *cailin*, I'm sorry. But that was not the right answer." Pulling out a gun from the back of his pants, he aimed it at her and without a moment's hesitation, she rolled, stood, and ran to the door. Eammon fired as she threw open the heavy oak, the bullet hitting her side.

Crying out in pain, the blinding snow storm and piercing cold took her breath away. Seeing an old tan Ford in the drive, she stumbled to the car, the blinding pain blurring her already clouded vision. Locking the doors as she got in, she found the keys tucked in the visor where Eammon's man kept them. Her hands shook as she tried three times to get the damn keys in the ignition. Finally, the old Ford started up.

Eammon's bodyguards ran out after her and banged on the rolled-up window, but she threw the car in gear and forced the pedal to the floor, skidding down the drive and eluding the body guards. She knew it was only a matter of time before they gave chase. She had to get the video uploaded. That was the mission. That video would put them all away for life.

The moon's rays were obscured by the snow clouds and the white flakes shown in her headlights. Her car swerved when the worn tires hit a patch of black ice.

The pain in her side grew more intense. She had to get help. Pulling out her cell phone, she dialed a number only to hear nothing as the call couldn't connect to a tower. Looking at the screen, she cursed the No Service icon at the top. But clicked over to the recording app. It was still recording.

"I hope this message gets to who it needs to. My name is Zoe Hanson I am an agent of the CIA. I don't know if I'll get out of this alive, but please tell my family I love them and not to cry. I pledged my loyalty to the United States of America and I am damn proud of that. I am uploading this in the hopes it reaches who it needs to. Steven, this is not your fault, don't you dare blame yourself. Tell that girlfriend of yours she's a lucky one and you will be a damn fine father. Brent is not to blame, he did not give me up. I'm going to sign off now and hope I can call with the Satellite phone. Find me, please."

She pressed upload and as the annoying circle went around and around and around waiting for a signal, she leaned over the gearshift, crying out when her side collided with the knob. The satellite phone was in the glove compartment. Dialing Steven's number, it rang. Rang. And rang.

"Dammit, answer!" she shouted.

"Phoenix?" his voice came over the receiver.

"Finally! Listen, Skylark is blown. He knows, Steven. He – shit!" she screamed when she saw the oncoming headlights of an eighteen-wheeler.

"Zoe? Zoe!" Steven shouted.

Chapter
Thirty-Eight

Jon and Courtney knocked on Dave's office door the next morning. As soon as Dave told them to come in, they sat down in the chairs opposite and waited. Dave looked different, a little ragged and his eyes were bloodshot as if he hadn't gotten any sleep that night before.

"Welcome back," Dave said. "How are you feeling, Courtney?"

"Better," she replied. "My headache is nearly gone."

"Good," he answered but there was little joy in the word. "Have you heard about the agent who was killed?"

"What agent?" Jon asked.

"Steven called me earlier this morning," he said. "It looks like one of his agents in the field was killed after she was made by Eammon O'Malley. This is what we were trying to warn you against."

"Jaysus," Jon breathed.

"I'm sorry, but I have no choice," Dave said. "Your badges and guns please. You are suspended until further notice."

"What? Why?" Jon demanded.

"Going against orders, putting lives at risk," he ticked off the offenses. "I warned you both."

"You did," Courtney agreed. "Can we know the name of the agent who was killed?"

"Zoe," Dave replied. "And Brent is unaccounted for."

Courtney let out a sigh. "Did she have any family?"

"Parents and a sister," he revealed. "They have been contacted."

Courtney closed her eyes and without another thought, she pulled out her gun and badge and handed them over. Dave nodded silently when they locked eyes and she walked out of the room through the adjoining door of her office.

Jon's gaze followed her then he turned to Dave. "I am sorry for Zoe, but you can't blame us, Dave," he said.

"The hell I can't," he snarked. "I told you not to go. Steven begged you to stop but you both decided to go after a lead. That is what got the agent killed and another MIA. Don't put this back on me. I told you not to do it. Now go."

Jon stood, pulled himself up to his full height and set his gun and badge next to Courtney's.

"I know there's more to this than that, when you're ready to tell me, you know where I'll be."

Dave didn't give anything away apart from a slight twitch in his left eye. Jon walked through to his office and gathered his things, meeting Courtney at the elevators. She was silent the whole ride down to the garage. When she hadn't spoken on the drive to his house, Jon finally broke the silence.

"I'm sorry, Courtney," he said. "I should have stopped while we were ahead. Now I've cost you your badge."

"You think that's why I'm upset?" She didn't turn to him. "We just cost a woman her life. Her parents have to bury their daughter. Her sister will never have her confidant, her best friend. We caused that. I think about what happened to me just a month ago and all I can think about is that I was given a second chance and I caused a woman to lose her life. What kind of monster does that?"

Jon pulled off the road, unbuckled his seat belt and pulled Courtney into him.

"Don't put that on you," he said. "It is on me."

"No, it's not," she replied. "We agreed together." Pulling away from him, she looked out the window. "Please just take me to my car. I want to go home."

Jon sighed heavily but sat back in his chair and drove them to his house. Without another word, Courtney got out of the car and walked to her Jeep. Getting in without looking back, she drove down the street and disappeared around the bend.

Walking into his house, Jon tossed his keys on the ledge and pulled off his shoes. Hearing Beth walk down the hall, he looked up. She was dressed in leggings and a long shirt, her hair was up in a sloppy bun and her glasses sat high on the bridge of her nose.

"Hey, what are you doing home so early? I thought you were at work," her soft voice comforted him.

"I was suspended," he finally admitted.

"What?" she breathed walking over to him and taking his hand. "What happened?" When she saw and felt the resignation in him, she ushered him to the sofa and poured him a cup of coffee. When she joined him, he finally launched into the story.

———⧓———

That next morning, Jon woke to the sound of his phone ringing. Clearing away sleep and easing Beth off his shoulder, he reached for the phone. An unknown number shown on the caller ID.

"Jonathan Greene," he answered.

"Jonathan," a woman's voice cooed on the other end. "It's so good to hear your voice again."

"Meredith," he spat.

"Now now, is that any way to speak to your son's wife?"

"*Ex*-wife," he stated.

"Still, semantics," she replied coyly. "I was enjoying watching you in Minneapolis. You left so suddenly. Tell me, is Courtney all right?"

"What do you want?" he demanded.

"To talk," she answered. "My friend Rob was excited for us

to meet. You know, he used to call me his Black Queen. He really wanted me to meet the Black King's Bishop and White Queen's Knight. Since Mat isn't here right now, how about we pick up where we left off all those years ago?"

"How about not?" Jon replied.

"Oh, come on," she whined. "For old times' sake. I know there's a few choice words you want to say to me. Well, this is your chance. But I know you're not stupid enough to come alone… or maybe you are. But I will tell you, you can bring that sexy little partner of yours if you want."

Jon hesitated for a moment but finally said, "where?"

"How about at Redorvsky's little cement plant?"

"No, neutral territory," he countered.

"Touchy," she clucked. "All right then, how about 1800 South Street. It's a storage facility. Number six. Ten o'clock?"

"Fine," Jon agreed.

"Oh good," she mocked. "Tell Scott I say hello, would you?"

Jon hung up on her and looked over at Beth who was wide awake and listening to the conversation.

"I know you're going to go," she started. "And you know I would never stop you, but do me a favor and don't go alone. Take Courtney. She'll back you up, please." Jon nodded silently. "And don't you dare get hurt. Do you understand? And call me."

Again, Jon nodded and pulled her into his arms. Kissing her hair, he got out of bed and went to the bathroom to call Courtney and shower.

Chapter Thirty-Nine

"I am very glad you called me, Jon," Courtney said as they drove. "I know it probably wasn't easy for you."

"Only because I want to keep you safe," he replied.

"I know, and I'm sorry I freaked out on you yesterday," she went on.

"I don't mind, you know that," he said.

"I do, but it's not fair to you," she answered. "I'm just thankful you didn't go alone to this. Even if we have no official back up, we need each other and I want to be there when this is all over. I need to see it to completion."

"So do I," he admitted. "Courtney... I need to talk to you anyway."

"Okay," she prompted.

"When we went to Ireland back in March, I realized just

how much I missed it and missed life with my mother and friends. I think the time has come I retire and move back home."

Courtney said nothing for a while. But when she did, she reached over and took his hand. "I know, Ryan and I already talked about that being a possibility. I support you. I will miss you like crazy but I support you nonetheless."

"I don't think I'll go back after our suspension is up," he said. "I've already talked to Beth about it and she wants to move too."

"Have you talked to Scott?"

"Not yet, but I have a feeling he may consider joining us over there."

"Well, I hope you all expect lots of visitors very often because I'm not going to be able to stay away," her voice broke.

"Hey," he shook her hand to make her look at him. "You are always welcome."

"Good," she took a deep breath. "Good."

Jon smiled softly at her just as the GPS announced they had reached their destination. Slowing, they found number six and parked the car.

Pulling out their spare guns, they silently told each other to be careful and turned to the door which was open a crack. Once inside, they scanned the darkened room, they saw and heard nothing until Meredith's voice boomed around the empty walls.

"Good of you to join me," she said. "Adam, the lights, please." The overhead fluorescent light bulb hummed and flickered on. "Well, good morning."

Looking around, they saw Adam Pellegrino on one side and Brent Tyler, a few bruises on his face but alive on the other side.

"Where are the others?" Jon asked.

"Others?" She questioned. "What others?"

"Redorvsky and O'Malley?" Courtney demanded.

"Look at you, little one," her words dripping with condescension. "I bet daddy is so proud. Aren't you, Jon?"

"What do you want, Meredith?" Jon demanded.

"Always so direct. There's never any foreplay with you Greene men, is there?" She chuckled and looked over at Adam. Jon watched her as she went to the table and poured a glass of wine.

"I know," she sighed as if she had seen him watching her. "Not exactly as you remember me, but I've learned a lot in the past eight years. Speaking of, how is my daughter?" Jon didn't answer and she shrugged. "It's not important. One thing I've learned is how to keep men under my spell." She took a slow drink of the wine, walked over to Brent and stroked his arm, trailing her fingers up to his neck and face. He leaned in and closed his eyes as if enjoying her touch. "So sorry, I didn't offer you any wine. Would you like some? It's five o'clock somewhere, right? Rather a fine vintage. But you would know I found it next to your aged whiskey bottle."

"Sorry, I didn't realize you came over, I would have fixed dinner," Jon snapped. She laughed a melodic tinkling laugh.

"Oh, how I've missed you," she said.

"Cut through the shit, Meredith," Jon stated. "What do you

want?"

"Hmm," she said and swallowed her wine. "I'm going to finish what Rob started. And when you're dead, I'm going to take my daughter back and in honor of Rob's dear friend Riley, I'm going to cut off your family by killing Scott, Kim and Ryan and have such pleasure while doing it."

"You'll have to kill me first," Jon said.

"Well, yes," she agreed. "That's why you're here. Sorry, did I forget to mention that?" She drained the wine and walked over to the table. Jon and Courtney raised their guns. Brent and Adam cocked theirs and aimed. "Not the face boys," she singed. "We do so want an open casket funeral, give Scott a chance to say goodbye."

"Just where do you think you're going?" Courtney asked as Meredith headed for the back door.

"Honey, I just bought this dress, I'm not going to get blood all over it. Clean up when you're done, Adam. Meet me at our place."

Adam nodded but held Courtney's gaze. Meredith slipped out the back door and it clanged shut. Four guns raised, four sets of eyes watching the others.

"Well, boys," Courtney said. "Looks like we got ourselves a little Mexican standoff."

"I don't know what your deal is with me, Pellegrino," Jon started. "But let Courtney go and we can discuss it rationally."

"I'm not going anywhere," Courtney replied. "But let's talk. Tell me, Adam, was she worth killing your brother, your wife?"

"And Brent, was it really worth getting Zoe killed?" Jon asked. Brent's eyes narrowed and flinched imperceptibly.

"We know you're in league with O'Malley and Redorvsky, so what is it? Gun running? Sex Trafficking?" Jon asked. "Where do I come into play?"

"You're the insurance we all need. We all have a beef with you and knowing you're dead will bring us that much closer," Adam replied. "So why don't you lower your gun, Lieutenant?"

"Didn't you hear?" Jon asked. "I'm suspended." Jon fired hitting Pellegrino in the shoulder. Courtney aimed at Brent who ducked and rolled into the shadows. Jon and Courtney took cover behind a few boxes as Pellegrino fired at them but missed by a mile.

"You might want to spend more time in the shooting range, Chief. Your aim is a little off." Jon taunted.

"I'll be sure to have your picture on the dummy," Pellegrino barked back.

"It doesn't have to be like this, Chief," Courtney called. "These people, Meredith, Redorvsky and O'Malley they don't care about you."

"Let me guess, and you do, Detective? Don't forget I'm a cop too. I know all the tactics," he yelled.

"I doubt you figured this one out," Brent's voice came from the shadows just before Jon and Courtney heard another shot. When there was silence, Jon peered over the boxes to see Brent standing over the body. "That was for Zoe." Jon stood and aimed his gun at Brent. Courtney stood beside him. Brent looked over at them and lowered his gun but they kept theirs trained on him. "Is it true? Is Zoe dead?" When Jon and Courtney didn't answer, he continued. "Oh, come on. You know who I am."

"Prove you're not a double agent," Jon replied.

"I can't," Brent stated holstering his gun. "But I can tell you Black King asked me to keep an eye on you."

Jon and Courtney glanced at each other. "How do we know you're telling the truth?" Courtney asked. "Who are you?"

"Don't you see the resemblance? Give me grey hair and make me twenty-five years older," Brent said.

Jon's eyes grew wide. "My god, Brent Weston?"

"Tyler, I took my mother's name," he answered.

"You're Dave's son?" Courtney asked.

"Guilty," he replied.

"Oh god, no wonder Dave was a wreck when I told you died."

"You told him I died?" Brent asked.

"When we went to the location you told Steven about and you weren't there, we thought for sure..." Jon's voice trailed off. "Jaysus, no wonder he was so messed up."

"It's kinda nice to hear my old man would miss me," Brent smiled. "Dad moved around a lot when I was a kid and my mom and stepdad raised me, but when I finally got to know him... he turned out to be a pretty cool guy. Always in the shadows, I guess that's why I chose that as my name. The Shadow. I'm the liaison between NSA, CIA and Homeland Security under my father."

Jon extended his hand to Brent. "Dave's mentioned you but honestly only after a couple beers I thought you died as a kid."

"Dad likes to keep it that way. The less anyone knows of our familial connection the better. He's always kept me at arm's length, it wasn't until I was older I understood that was his way of showing me he loved me. He didn't want anything to happen to me because of his work. I should call him. I'm not sure if Steven—" a shot rang out and Brent pitched forward, the bullet grazing his arm. Jon and Courtney immediately raised their guns. Jon helped Brent behind the boxes.

"I'm okay," Brent said inspecting the burned graze. "That's gotta be Meredith, we left everyone else behind in Minneapolis."

"I always knew you were a plant, pretty boy," Meredith called out from the shadows, her voice vibrated around the empty unit making it difficult to know where she was.

"Stay here, cover me," Jon whispered to Courtney. She nodded and Jon eased out from behind the boxes and made his way silently down the side of the unit, staying in the shadows. Just as his eyes adjusted to the darkness, he saw the glint of a barrel pointed where Courtney and Brent waited but to Jon's horror, Courtney was cautiously looking over the boxes in an effort to cover him. Meredith's sick grin reflected in the dim light and all Jon saw was Carol looking over the crates.

A voice foreign to his own shouted at Courtney to get down. She turned to look at him but he took off running directly into Meredith's path. His legs felt like they were trending through a peat bog. He had to get to her. He had to save her this time. Courtney's big blue eyes turned into Carol's dark brown and he felt her last breaths on his lips again, felt her heart stop beating as he held her to him, the pain of having lost the one person that meant more to him than anything. She was there for him to save and he wasn't going to screw up again.

Jon turned when he heard the two shots, felt the blood splatter on him but he refused to think he was too late. He stumbled to Courtney, so grateful she was alive. He fell over her, then the world went black.

Chapter
Forty

Jon was standing on a beach. It was dusk, warm, he felt the sand beneath his bare feet. Looking down, he wore his favorite linen pants and Tommy Bahama shirt. Gazing out at the crystal blue water of the Caribbean, he smiled slightly and raised his head toward the sun, closed his eyes. The warmth was comforting and he breathed in the salty air.

The silence was calming as the waves crashed against the shore in their usual rhythmic melody. The seagulls in their obsessive search for food was the only other sound and he felt at peace, a peace he had never felt.

Slowly walking forward, he began to remember where he was. When they were on the yacht for their honeymoon, he had stopped off at a small island where he and Carol had spent the day alone, making love on the beach and sunbathing together before having dinner on the yacht. Before him was the outcropping of rocks and an archway cutting through. He smiled when he remembered how they ran over that way to get out of the afternoon cloudburst and wound up making out against the rocks. He walked through the arch touching the stones gently.

Rounding a bend in the beach, he stopped suddenly. A little way ahead of him was a woman. She stood at the edge of the dry white sand looking out at the sea. She wore a white linen sundress that buttoned up the bodice. Her tanned arms were crossed over her chest, her loose brown hair blew in the warm wind and her dress flapped around her equally tanned legs.

He blinked a few times to make sure she was there. Then he took off running.

"Carol!" He shouted as he ran.

The woman turned when she heard her name and ran a hand through her hair holding it back from her face as the wind blew. Her eyes grew large with surprise when she saw him coming toward her.

"Jonny?" she whispered.

He reached her then and picked her up, twirling her around. He was laughing as he set her down and eagerly kissed her. He didn't pull back until Carol gently pushed him away and looked up into his green eyes.

"Jonny?" she asked again.

"Have I changed so much, baby?" he teased leaning down and kissing her again.

"What are you doing here?" she pleaded.

"What do you mean?" he asked.

Before she could say anything, they heard a voice calling from a bungalow he hadn't seen before.

"Carol, darlin' tea's up, do you want it outside?"

The voice had a familiar Irish ring to it. Jon looked at her questioning.

"That's fine," she called back.

Looking toward the bungalow, he could hardly believe his eyes when his father, just as he remembered him walked out carrying a tea tray. A young girl about twelve years old followed him.

"It's so beautiful but I tell ya it's a heat wave to be sure. Why couldn't we—" He cut off when he saw Jon. "Jonny boy?" The young girl looked up at him.

"Who is it, grandpa?" she asked.

"What are you doing here?" Patrick asked.

"What's going on?" Jon replied.

"Jonny," Carol started. "You shouldn't be here. What happened to you?"

"I was with Courtney we were in a storage unit and I was running to save her… but…" he took a deep breath, his eyes trailing from Carol to his father then down to the little girl with his green eyes. "Care, what's going on?"

"Jonny… you're dying."

"Don't you dare do this to me, Jon!" Courtney shouted as she frantically performed CPR on Jon's still form. Everything had happened so fast when Meredith fired and Jon fell on top of her, Courtney tried to get up but couldn't shift Jon's weight. With Brent's help, she could move him but Brent went after Meredith who again ran out the back door. Courtney called 9-1-1 and told them what happened as she checked for a pulse. When she couldn't find one, she immediately started CPR.

"Come on," she shouted. "Don't you die on me, do you hear me? Come on!" She stopped to give mouth-to-mouth and checked his pulse, still nothing. "No, come on, you wake up you hear me?" a few more compressions on his chest and another round of mouth-to-mouth and the EMTs raced in. She fell back as two men approached.

"Two GSWs to the chest about five minutes ago, I have been performing CPR since," she explained.

"Are you hurt?" one of them asked.

"No," she shook her head realizing she must have Jon's blood on her. The EMTs went to work on Jon but their faces were grim.

"Come on, Jon, please, don't leave me, don't leave Scott and Ryan, please," she whispered next to him. Knowing it was only a minute or so later, even though it felt like hours, her body went cold when one EMT stopped and looked at the other, shaking his head.

"No!" Courtney screamed. "No, keep working. He's a stubborn jackass but he'll live, he has to."

"He's gone," one of the EMTs said.

"No!" she raced to him and started CPR again. "Come on, you selfish bastard, wake up. Live, damn you!" she felt the EMTs hands on her, trying to pull her away but she wasn't having it. "Just a little longer. Come on," she bent down and did mouth-to-mouth again. "Jon, I know you want to stay, I know you're with Carol, but we need you here first. Don't do this. Don't do this to Scott. You can't leave me, do you hear? You can't! I won't let you!"

Courtney's vision was blurring with tears but she still pounded on Jon's chest hoping, praying for a miracle.

———

Scott let out a painful breath as if he were punched in the gut. Kim and Alex looked over at him as he hunched over the boardroom table breathing heavily.

"Scott?" Kim rushed to him. "Are you okay?"

"Can't breathe," he said. Kim pushed him back in the chair and Alex loosened his tie and collar buttons. Tears started racing down his cheeks and he didn't know why.

"Are you hurt? What's going on?" Kim examined him, not seeing any wound.

"I don't know," Scott replied. "Just suddenly I couldn't breathe and I felt such sadness, emptiness... oh god, dad."

Chapter
Forty-One

"You have to live do you hear me?" Courtney kept the compressions going even after the EMTs tried to pull her off of him. "Come on, come on!"

Lowering over him again, she put her ear to his lips trying to feel a breath. Covering his mouth with hers and pinching his nose, she tried to breathe for him. Checking his pulse, she cursed him again when there was nothing beneath her fingertips.

"No!" she screamed but this time she didn't try to stop the EMTs from pulling her back. She fell back and cried out pressing a shaking hand to her lips and nose. Her hands were covered with his blood but she didn't care. The EMTs were trying to soothe her with encouraging words and words of sympathy but she wasn't having it. "You lied to me!" she screamed at Jon's body. "You swore you would always be there for me! You swore! And you lied!" She lunged forward and hit his chest with her fist. "I'm so sorry." She wept throwing herself over his chest. "Please don't go. Not yet." Crying over him, not listening to the EMTs conversation about calling the M.E., her sobs stopped so abruptly the men turned to her.

"Jon?" she questioned then lowered her ear to his chest again and cried out. "Please! Help! His heart is beating again."

The EMTs looked at each other then rushed to Jon's side where they felt for a pulse. Sure enough, it was light but it was there. Jon was alive.

"Courtney!" She heard Scott yell. Turning, Scott, Ryan, Kim and Beth ran up to her.

"Scott! Oh, thank God," he hugged her then looked down at her shirt.

"Oh my god, is that all dad's?" he asked seeing the blood stains.

She nodded and looked over at Beth who was as pale as a ghost.

"What happened?" Kim asked. "All we know is what you told Scott when you called."

"We were in a storage unit and there was a shootout. Jon jumped in front of me," Courtney explained. "He was shot twice."

"Where?" Ryan asked.

"The chest," she replied.

Everyone was silent for a moment until Beth stepped

forward, "is he alive?" was all she could ask.

"Yes," Courtney replied. "The EMTs stopped working on him, thinking he was dead but I didn't give up on him. His heart started beating again but when we were in the ambulance, he flatlined again. They were able to revive him and have him in surgery now."

"Who shot him?" Scott demanded.

Courtney didn't want to answer at first and it must have shown on her face because Scott took another step closer to her and demanded again. "Who, Courtney?"

"Easy, man," Ryan quieted.

"We have been following this case since Riley and then Rob, now it seems another has tried to take over their mission," she explained.

"Who did it?" Scott questioned.

"Meredith," she replied. It took Scott a second to figure it out, but when he did, his face turned red with rage and had Ryan not pulled him away, Courtney was sure he would have punched a wall.

"Do you know the surgeon?" Kim asked when the women were alone.

"I haven't seen him before, but I know the name," Courtney replied. "I'm sure he'll be all right. I'll ask when Ryan gets back."

"I want the best," Beth said.

"I know you do, Beth, so do I," Courtney took her hand in hers and gave it a reassuring squeeze.

Ryan walked back to them without Scott. "He's on the phone with Uncle Rick," Ryan explained. "Where was Uncle Jon shot?"

"The chest, not sure about the rest," she replied. "Montgomery is the surgeon."

"He's good," Ryan put Beth's fears at ease. "He'll do well."

"They gave me this and asked me to wait," Courtney showed the buzzer given to family and friends of patients in surgery.

"Have you eaten?" Ryan asked.

"I can't," she replied. "I wish I had a change of clothes."

"I have a shirt in my locker, wait here," Ryan offered and disappeared down the hallway.

———◦◦———

It was nearly seven hours later when the buzzer in Beth's hand went off telling them the doctor was ready to see them. Terrified of bad news, everyone piled into the small waiting room office. Rick and Jenny had arrived a short time ago and stood together, holding a sleeping Sarah. Kathleen and Keelan were in the air on their way but wouldn't land for another few minutes in Philadelphia. Ryan sat beside Courtney and her parents, his Notre Dame t-shirt baggy on her.

Finally, the door opened and two doctors walked in. One Courtney had only seen briefly as Jon was wheeled into the ER and the other was Ryan's mentor; Fred Sullivan. Ryan stood from the couch and walked up beside his cousin.

"Ryan," Fred greeted with his usual cool confidence.

"Mr. Greene?" the other doctor asked. Scott nodded. "I'm Dr. Montgomery, I performed your father's emergency surgery."

"He's alive?" Scott asked.

"He is," the doctor replied. "The surgery was a success. We were able to save him, but he has a long road to recovery ahead of him."

The exhale of relief nearly moved the doctors' hair. Scott bent over and placed his hands on his knees, breathing deliberately so as not to pass out. Kim stroked calming circles on his back. Beth gasped in joy and Courtney took her hand.

"When can we see him?" Courtney asked, her shaky voice betraying her own relief.

"He's in recovery, it was a tough time, I'll not lie," Dr. Montgomery explained. "We nearly lost him a couple times, but he is currently stable. One bullet lodged in his sternum preventing it from doing any real damage. The other one collapsed his lung and nicked his aortic artery. He's a fighter. It was clear he wasn't ready to die yet."

"Thank you, Kevin," Ryan shook his hand. "I appreciate it."

"Fred's keen eye and determination is what kept your uncle alive, Ryan. After the fourth flatline, I wasn't sure we were going to make it," Dr. Montgomery said.

Ryan turned to his mentor and with a quick glance at Dr. Montgomery, who nodded as everyone thanked him again and slipped out of the room, Ryan embraced his mentor tightly.

"Thank you," he said.

"Of course," Fred replied then pulled back. "Though I am getting a little tired of saving the men in your family," he winked.

"Trust me, we're tired of seeing the inside of this hospital," Scott answered, now his father was going to be all right, his joy overflowed.

"When he's out of recovery, we'll call for you," Fred explained. "Until then, get something to eat, call your family, he's all right."

"Thank you," Ryan said again and the answering appreciation from everyone else echoed in the small room.

Scott's phone rang and he quickly pulled it out. "It's mam." He answered it. "Mam? The doctor just left, he's alive."

Chapter
Forty-Two

"Dad?" Scott called to Jon as he rested on the hospital bed. "Dad, can you hear me?" there was, of course, no response. "I don't know if you can, I know sometimes they say people can hear you." He pulled a chair up beside the bed. "I need you to wake up. It's already been long enough. I know you've been through hell but don't leave me. I know you've seen mom, okay? But I'm not ready to give up. You have to wake up.

"You remember when I was ten and I fell from the tree out in front of the ranch? You remember how you knew my leg was broken but you didn't want me to see it. You took me in your arms and held me against you. I never felt so safe. It gave me the strength I needed to get through the pain. You held me until the ambulance came. I remember, I wouldn't let you go, even when you told me it was all right. I needed them to take me, mom was right there but I hung on to you. You remember that? You swore you would always be there for me... I'm begging you now, make good on your promise. Don't leave me when I need you here the most. Please fight. Fight for me... please."

Scott lowered his head to his dad's forearm. Tears ran down his cheeks. It had been five days and Jon had yet to wake up. Though his vitals were fine, Ryan and Fred agreed it might take another couple days, but Scott knew why. Jon was with Carol and he didn't want to leave. His tears continued to flow, not having cried so much in a long time, his stomach was in knots. Then finally, a hand stroked the back of his head.

"Shh, shh, Scottie, I'm okay."

Scott lifted his head so fast it spun. Looking over at Jon, he let out a soft groan when he saw his dad's eyes open, looking at him.

"I'll always be here for you," Jon said softly.

"Oh my god," Scott cried and threw his arms around his father. "I was so worried about you."

"I'm all right," Jon promised. "You can't get rid of me that easily."

"Never," Scott assured. "I'm so glad you're awake."

"Is Courtney okay?" Jon asked.

"She's fine," Scott answered. "Scared for you but she's all right. Everyone's outside." Jon winced when he tried to take a deep breath. "Let me call the nurse and then get Beth. I asked for a moment alone but she's been here with you the whole time."

Scott reached over for the nurse call button and rushed to

the door. "He's awake."

Everyone stumbled over each other trying to get to the door.

"Excuse me, being his mother has privileges," Jon heard his mother's voice say. Chuckling then groaning, he looked over to see her pushing her way past everyone. Beth was next in, followed by Courtney and Keelan.

"Oh Jaysus, Mary, and Joseph, thank the Lord!" his mother cried and ran to his side.

"I'm all right," Jon said as she peppered his face with kisses. Beth leaned forward and kissed him full on the lips.

"Thank god," Beth breathed.

"Hey, baby," he answered. "Sorry I didn't call."

She left out a tearful laugh but kissed him again.

"Where's my partner?" Jon asked.

"I'm here," Courtney said from behind his mother.

"Hey, you okay?" he asked. She nodded and sniffled.

"Don't you ever do that to me again, do you understand?" she cried. "I thought I lost you."

"I'm okay," he reached for her, the IV in his hand making it difficult but as soon as his mother stepped back, Courtney raced to his side.

A sharp two knocks echoed in the room and Scott let the person in. Ryan and a nurse walked in along with Dr. Fred Sullivan.

"Well, Mr. Greene," Fred began, rubbing his hands together to dry the foam hand sanitizer he sprayed before he walked in. "I'm glad you're awake. I hope you don't mind, I have asked my

Assistant Head of Surgery to join me today."

Courtney whirled around just to see Ryan's grin. "Surprise," he said. "They offered me the job this morning."

General congratulations and a squeal from Courtney as she ran into his arms, bounced around the room. But Fred walked over to Jon and looked at the machines.

"Well, it looks like your vitals are stable," Fred said. "Let's order more blood workup and make sure his counts are where they should be. Also, I want to schedule an MRI to check for any internal bleeding." Ryan was writing down everything as Fred spoke with a side wink at Courtney. "We'll get the tests ordered and leave you to it. Though I completely understand why you're all in here now, I do have ask you to limit your visits. He needs his rest."

"We will, thank you, Doctor," Beth replied.

"Can I talk to Courtney for a moment?" Jon asked everyone.

"Of course," Kathleen said with one final kiss to her son's forehead and ushered everyone out.

Once they were alone, Courtney pulled up a chair and sat beside Jon's bed. He looked over at her. "Brent?"

"Flesh wound," she confirmed. "He's okay. He and Steven have gone silent. No one knows where he is."

"What about Meredith?" Jon asked.

"Brent went after her, I don't know," she answered. "But I did have to tell Scott. He wouldn't let it drop."

"Shite," Jon muttered. "That's okay. He was going to figure it out sooner or later. He didn't take it well, I imagine."

"Not well at all."

"Any word from Dave?"

"I called him and told him. In his words, 'damn you, gunny for getting yourself shot.' Then he swore to come see you soon."

"Sounds about right," Jon replied. Then after a long pause, he took her hand in his and squeezed. "You remember what I told you I was thinking about earlier?"

"Retiring?" she offered. Jon nodded.

"I think this has shown me where I need to be," he said. "I doubt I'll be fit enough to be a cop again."

"I figured you'd say that," Courtney looked down. "With Ryan's new job and my family here, I don't know if we can follow but I will miss you all like crazy."

"We'll visit more often than not," Jon said. "Maybe one of these days you will all move to the best place on earth."

"I'd be all for it, so long as my family would come too," she replied. "But enough of that. Concentrate on getting healthy."

Before Jon could answer, there was a knock at the door. When Jon called for the person to come in, he smiled when he saw his brother. Rick took a deep breath and let it out in a rush.

"Thank god," he breathed.

"I'll give you guys a moment," Courtney smiled, then turning back to Jon she squeezed his hand. "I'm beyond glad you're okay."

"Me too," he replied. Courtney left the room and Rick stepped forward.

"I'm sorry I wasn't here," Rick started. "Sarah needed to sleep so I took her and Jenny back to the hotel."

"Hotel?" Jon asked. "You don't need to stay at a hotel. You know you can always stay at the house. I know you don't need the added expense right now."

"To hell with expenses," Rick's voice was low. "My baby brother was in the hospital, I wasn't about to be at a place further than running distance."

Jon bit back his next words and merely nodded. "I'm glad you're here."

"You can never do that to me again, all right?" Rick said. "When Scott called, I honestly thought I was going to lose it. You're my baby brother, you can't go before me."

"Hey hey, nobody's going anywhere," Jon reached for him knowing he would never ask for a hug and pulled him down embracing him tightly.

"I love you, Jon, we're all we have left."

"I love you too, Rick," he replied. When he pulled back, Rick looked down at him. "I wanted to talk to you anyway."

"What about?" Rick asked sitting down.

"I think I'm going to retire and move back home," he said.

Rick leaned back in the chair and nodded. "I just mentioned the same thing to Jenny not two days ago. I want Sarah to grow up like we did. She deserves to be home."

"With mom getting on in years I want to be sure I'm there for her."

"I understand," Rick said. "Do you think we could rent Kathleen's old cottage on the land?"

"You're welcome in the house," Jon replied.

"Aye, but I think Jenny and I will want our privacy sometimes," he winked. Jon laughed and promptly groaned.

"Arse, don't make laugh," Jon moaned. Rick grinned and patted his brother's hand.

The brothers sobered for a long moment, the seriousness of their situation weighing heavily.

"I miss Ireland," Jon said.

"Me too."

Jon turned to him and took his hand. "Let's go home, brother."

Chapter
Forty-Three

Steven lowered the binoculars from his eyes after seeing Meredith walk into the store in Madrid, Spain. He turned to Brent who nodded slightly.

They both got out of the car and headed toward the store. Speaking Spanish to each other so as not to draw too much attention to themselves, though they were two good looking men in a women's boutique. The woman behind the counter greeted them and as planned, Brent went over to her and spoke low, saying he was looking for an anniversary gift for his girlfriend as Steven walked around the small store looking for Meredith.

When he had made a lap without seeing her, he passed Brent, engaging with the shop keeper explaining the body of his *girlfriend* in order to pick the right lingerie. Seeing the two other women in the store toward the front, he slipped through the curtain partitioning off the dressing room. One curtain was pulled closed. Steven took his gun and screwed on the silencer, then slowly tipped the side of the curtain back only slightly to confirm it was Meredith inside.

Tugging the curtain back, he didn't give her time to scream. He pulled the trigger and watched the life drain from Meredith's eyes as she slid down the mirrored wall to the floor. Closing the curtain, Steven replaced his gun and walked back out, as soon as the coast was clear. Brent was at the register, paying for what looked like a very skimpy red lace garterslip and bustier. Steven stepped outside and waited for him to finish. When Brent walked out, they headed to the car and he passed Steven the frilly pink bag. Steven raised an eyebrow.

"Happy engagement," Brent winked. "Though I think it's more a gift to you. Enjoy."

They got in the SUV and Steven set the bag aside. Pulling out of the street parking space, Brent grabbed his phone and called a number.

"Boss," Brent said into the phone when Dave answered. "It's done."

"Good," Dave answered. "Steven did you get a chance to talk to Mat?"

"Last night. How's Jon?"

"He's alive, woke up this morning," Dave explained.

"Good, I gave Mat the burner. I'll call him."

"Do, and then get back here. You boys have earned a couple

weeks off."

"What about Paris, Dad?" Brent asked. "You promised."

"I did," he replied. "As long as we're back before Redorvsky's, Pellegrino's and O'Malley's trials we're good to go."

"Think we got them this time?"

"Zoe's video uploaded to the cloud when she... when she ran off the road. She died getting us this information. We got them. And the DA and I have a secret weapon."

Steven nodded. "We'll be on the next flight out."

"I'll meet you at the airport." Dave hung up and Steven drove to the airport as Brent purchased their tickets for the next available flight.

Chapter
Forty-Four

Two months later...

"All rise, this court is now in session, Judge Tamara Williams presiding," the bailiff said as the judge entered the courtroom and sat down at the bench. Scott leaned over to his dad as the judge called the court to order.

"I've worked with her in the past," he whispered. "She's tough but fair."

"I'd feel better if you were up there instead of the DA," Jon answered.

"Me too but she'll do great," Scott promised. "She just has to play to the heartstrings of the jury with that tape from the agent and she'll have it in the bag."

As the trial went on, both sides volleyed, argued, interviewed, summarized, objected and played to the jury. Ryan started nodding off after the fifth hour but Scott had to restrain himself from objecting. The DA was letting things slide and it worried him. But finally, the judge announced,

"Counsellor, call your last witness."

The DA stood and addressed the judge. "Your honor, my final witness is running a little late. I would request a five minute recess until he arrives."

"You are sure he'll be here in that time?" the judge asked.

"I believe—" the DA was cut off when the door opened and a messenger came in going to the attorney. The DA sighed in relief and nodded. "Your honor, my witness has arrived and at this time wishes to invoke his right to a closed court room."

"Who does he wish to leave, counsellor?"

"All media personnel and anyone unrelated to the case, excluding," she put on her glasses and read. "Those related to the victim or victims, Jonathan Greene and family, and any and all officers of the law."

Jon's brows furrowed and he looked over at Scott who shrugged. Those the DA asked to leave, gathered their things as the judge agreed and ordered them out. Once the door was closed again, the judge had the DA proceed.

"Your honor, I am very happy to be able to call, Viktor Viktorovich Redorvsky, *son* of the accused to the stand," she announced.

"No," Jon breathed. A side door opened and Viktor walked in along with Keelan. His steps faltered for a moment when he saw Jon but he quickly recovered and walked down the aisle ignoring his father's murderous glare. Keelan slipped in beside Jon.

"What's going on?" Jon whispered.

"Later," Keelan answered.

"Mr. Redorvsky," the DA began after Viktor was sworn in. "Let's start with the most obvious question... where have you been?"

Jon, Scott, Ryan, Keelan, and Viktor walked out of the courthouse and breathed in the hot July air. They stood at the Indianapolis Courthouse steps where it all began.

"Well," Viktor started. "At least I know I did my part."

"They're all going away for a long time thanks to you," Scott replied.

"Lock him up and throw away the key, I say," Viktor said. "Do you think Sergei will be all right?"

Sergei had received a much lighter sentence thanks to Viktor's testimony but he was still going away for ten years."

"I'm sure he'll be fine," Jon squeezed Viktor's shoulder. "And you'll be there for him when he gets out."

Viktor nodded. "I'll miss him. He told me not to come visit, but I'm still going to write. I know he'll probably not be able to write back. You don't think they'll put him in the same prison as my father, do you?"

"That's up to the courts," Scott said.

"I hope not. Dad would have us both killed as soon as possible if he could."

"I wondered why you refused Marshals," Jon harrumphed as they walked down the steps to his car.

"Because no one knows where I've been," Viktor said. "And I wasn't about to make my life more of circus."

"Then let's get you in safe," Jon said opening the door. "I'm glad to see you again, Viktor."

"I'm glad you're okay, Jon," he answered, closing the door as he sat next to Scott. "And it's nice to use my own name again."

"I'm sure you are," Jon replied. "Now how about dinner?"

Epilogue

Alleen Caiseal, County Clare, Ireland
Six months later...

It was late, well passed the usual time to go to bed. Jon, Beth, Ryan, Courtney, Kathleen, Keelan, Mat, Connie, Iollan, Viktor, Patrick, Jenny, Steven, Amber, Mark and his boyfriend Spencer passed around a final couple bottles of champagne, filling their glasses. Seeing Scott and Kim saying goodnight to the last guests, they handed the bride and groom a glass and toasted.

"To you both," Jon started. "As you start your lives together as husband and wife all I can say is, it's about damn time."

"I'll drink to that," Beth teased raising her glass.

"You've been saving that one, haven't you?" Scott laughed as they drank.

"For about twenty years," Jon winked. "I worked hard on my speech earlier, this one not so much."

"Oh, that reminds me," Mat pulled out a small gift wrapped in a white and ivory wrapping paper. "I asked Jon to get this for me in case I wasn't here for your wedding. I'm glad I am able to give it to you." He handed Scott the gift. Scott looked over at Jon who winked and wrapped his arm tighter around Beth. Scott opened it and froze.

"What is it, baby?" Kim asked.

"Is this…" Scott breathed looking up at his uncle. Mat nodded.

"Your great-grandfather's ivory handled rancher knife. His initials are engraved there. CB. You're named after him. Charles Bernardo," Mat explained. "Your mother always loved it even as a little girl. Just before he died, he gave it to her. She used it sparingly but always said when she had a son of her own she would not only name him after her favorite grandfather but also give him the knife on his wedding day." Scott was silent for a moment. "She always wanted to be here. She dreamed of this day for you. I can't bring your mother here today, but I can give you this part of her."

Scott looked up at his uncle, tears swimming in his eyes. "Thank you."

Mat broke away from Connie and gave him a hug. "I love you, my little rancher."

Scott breathed a laugh. Mat hadn't called him his unique nickname for a long time.

"Ugh, enough tears," Scott said, wiping his eyes. "Thank you, *Tio*. The best gift." Mat winked and took his champagne glass back from his date.

"More champagne," Jon called. As the other bottles were

opened and most of their glasses were topped off, Scott wrapped his arm around Kim's waist and she nodded.

"Well, I - *we* want to thank you all for helping us plan this, getting everyone here and making it a success. My wife and I... my wife, I really love that," Scott pulled Kim into him and kissed her hair. "My beautiful wife and I are eternally grateful. Dad, we couldn't have done it without you and I am so glad we don't have to. Beth, thank you for this amazing woman. You gave her to me in marriage today and I swear to protect, love and care for her. She is truly the love of my life. To my new brothers," he turned to Steven and Mark. "You have my permission to kick my ass if I ever hurt her."

"Oh, trust me, we will," Steven replied.

"You hurt him, you'll have to deal with me," Kim said.

"Ah no fair, baby sis," Mark whined.

"I'll keep him in line, sweetheart," Spencer replied resting his arm on Mark's shoulder. They had been dating for nearly a year, but Mark had not come out to his family until three weeks ago. Since then, Spencer had been a staple in their lives and had become one of the family.

"I'm glad y'all stayed because we wanted to share a special moment with you all," Scott said. "Dad, Kim and I have talked it over and we have decided we want to join you and Beth here. I've already talked to Alex, he's ready to buy the firm and we will move to Ireland."

"Ah grand, that's great," Jon beamed, pulling his son in for a hug.

"I want to work the land, hand in hand with Iollan," Scott said. "I think it's time we Greenes came home."

"You won't be taking over for me until you have a son," Jon teased. "Don't try and weed me out just yet."

"Well," Scott continued. "That brings me to our *other* announcement." He pulled Kim into him tighter.

"No," Jon breathed before laughing and cheering. "Really?"

"Kim and I are expecting our first child on July Fourth," Scott stated.

Shouts and applauds went up around the room. Jon pulled his son into a hug as Beth grabbed Kim to her.

"Oh, sweetheart," Beth framed her daughter's face. "The best happiness to you. Your wish has finally come true."

Kim nodded as her eyes filled with tears. "Mama, is this real?"

"Yes, darling," she confirmed. "It's real. It's absolutely real. I love you so much."

"Love you too," she cried and hugged her mother.

Jon held his son tightly but before he pulled back, he kissed his cheek and said, "I'm so proud of you, son. Everything you went through has led to this moment. Congratulations. I love you and I can't wait for the future with your son, my grandson," Jon's voice choked on the last word. "Thank God it's all over and finally a happy ending."

The End

Acknowledgements

Wow... it's over. The end of an era. I won't lie, I cried. Listening to my favorite Irish tune, *Parting Glass* that randomly began playing on my music. The journey I started in 2003 in eighth grade and pursued in 2012, has come to an end, with this third and final installment of the *Greene and Shields Files*. Thank you all who have been with me from the beginning. Their story is over, the characters have finished talking to me. Putting so much of me in each character, it's difficult when the story ends. I hope you have enjoyed this trilogy as much as I have. These characters will always be nearest and dearest to my heart as they were truly the first characters to tell me their story and ones I could get lost in. I love them all dearly but it's time to let them go.

I would love to hear from you! Please considering posting a review or connecting with me on Facebook or Twitter.

If you enjoyed the *Greene and Shields Files* as much as I did and would like to read more about different characters, please consider contacting me for *Tales from the Heart*. These short novelettes finish the stories of minor characters and visits the best day of Courtney's life as well as a sneak peek of a future Christmas for the beloved characters. This will not be sold in any stores and the only way to receive a paperback is by contacting me at any of my events or through my website: www.mkatherineclark.net

Thank you so much and thank you, Jon and Courtney for choosing me to tell your story. You will be greatly missed.

Made in the USA
Monee, IL
20 June 2021